Kaleidoscope Anthology 2003

Kaleidoscope Anthology 2003

Mother Margaret and the Rhinoceros Café

Editors:
Frank Symons and Radhika Sekar

Kaleidoscope Books

Editors: Frank Symons & Radhika Sekar
Kaleidoscope Books, RR #5, Perth, ON. K7H 3C7. Canada
kaleidoscopebooks@rogers.com

These stories are reprinted with the permission of the authors who retain the copyrights to their stories. "Incident at 33" by James Romanow was first published in Storyteller Winter 2003. "Mangohatten" by James Romanow was first published in FreeFall Magazine (Calgary).

Cover Design: David Badour, 44 Hobart Crescent Ottawa. K2H 5S4

Winners of Kaleidoscope Contest 2003: Timothy Kaiser (1 st Prize), James Romanow (2nd Prize), Rosemary McCracken (3 rd Prize). Honourable Mentions: Ken Loomes, Mark Foss, James Romanow, Sheila Howe, Angelo Eidse and Cecilia Kennedy.

Acknowledgements: We wish to thank Cyril Dabydeen, Andrew Dutton, Brian Murray and Nik Haramis for their valuable input and assistance.

Printed in Victoria, Canada

National Library of Canada Cataloguing in Publication

Mother Margaret and the Rhinoceros Cafe : Canadian stories of race, religion, and cultural conflict in a globalized world / F.S. Symons, editor, Radhika Sekar, co-editor.

ISBN 1-4120-0542-6

1. Canada—Ethnic relations—Fiction. 2. Culture conflict—Canada—Fiction. 3. Short stories, Canadian (English) 4. Canadian fiction (English) I. Symons, F. S. (Frank S.), 1940- II. Sekar, Radhika, 1946-

PS8321.M68 2003   C813'.0108355   C2003-903804-1

TRAFFORD

This book was published *on-demand* in cooperation with Trafford Publishing. On-demand publishing is a unique process and service of making a book available for retail sale to the public taking advantage of on-demand manufacturing and Internet marketing. **On-demand publishing** includes promotions, retail sales, manufacturing, order fulfilment, accounting and collecting royalties on behalf of the author.

Suite 6E, 2333 Government St., Victoria, B.C. V8T 4P4, CANADA
Phone   250-383-6864   Toll-free   1-888-232-4444 (Canada & US)
Fax   250-383-6804   E-mail   sales@trafford.com
Web site   www.trafford.com   TRAFFORD PUBLISHING IS A DIVISION OF TRAFFORD HOLDINGS LTD.
Trafford Catalogue #03-0911   www.trafford.com/robots/03-0911.html

10   9   8   7   6   5   4   3

CONTENTS

Introduction

I love the contrast between whimsical playfulness and lurking danger in Tim Kaiser's "Mother Margaret and The Rhinoceros Café"—how a Dene settlement springs to life in a dozen sentences, the plot deploys around one mesmerizing character with nothing more than voice and desire, and magic happens. Single mother Margaret takes on the elders and the entire village to realize her dream. The point of view shifts neatly back and forth between the white male teacher and Mother Margaret. Her heartbreaking inner conflict runs parallel to the plot as humour and love flood the story, and resentment and envy "whistle in the background."

Amazingly, love also floods James Romanow's "Incident on 33" in an office building. Points of view clash on "infidels", "a good marriage", office politics and elitist power. In terms of family conflicts, Anita Rau Badami's work comes to mind. A forbidden love affair ignites emotions, complicated by a triangle comprising a "high cheek-boned, blonde" female vice-president, a male Muslim trader "whose daily work counted in the millions," and a beautiful Hindu woman. Human nature is embodied in sexual energies as love seems to merge with hate, and tensions steadily rise. These subplots dovetail into the central, lascivious, video-like sensual relationship. "She wore a smile he knew from school, the small, knowing smirk found famously on the Mona Lisa. She licked her spoon clean of the yoghurt . . . They walked back, his thumbs caressing, following the cleft down . . .."

Rosemary McCracken's "Crazy" shows how would-be Canadians play a psychological end-game in the sinister and shadowy world of illegal immigrants and false papers, recalling Catherine Bush's most recent novel. The Quran forbids alcohol, but this and other precepts are swept aside, and, in thriller style, one of them is inexorably backed into a corner. The tough ending leaves the reader pondering the issues for a long time.

Love reappears in Ken Loomes' story "Pokey's Christmas Cookies" about the dysfunctional family and a bright kid's struggle against evil. "He turned just a little so he could see her out of the corner of his eye . . . . She was always looking over to see if he was watching her but she would move her shoulders first just a bit . . . ." How Tolstoy-like, the detailed use of body language to get a point across!

"Circumcision Through Words" by Mark Foss is a daring foray into cultural antagonism at the cutting edge, reminiscent of Alan Cumyn. It pits Afro-Canadians against each other: "Who are you to blame the mothers? ... Who would you blame then? The fathers?" The narrator handles his characters and subject with great delicacy. The tension grabs the reader and will not let go while in parallel the narrator experiences his own seemingly unrelated problems. Yet main plot and subplot mirror each other in understated ways.

Cecilia Kennedy's "Welcome to Mill Street" reflects tensions in a street in any large Canadian city. Told with a sly humour, it has the feel of Stuart McLean's books and CBC program. A house is sold, and the neighbours speculate about the new owner. "I pictured a family with eleven kids. Hells Angels. A Mormon with three wives." The surprises keep coming right up until the startling end.

"Abe" by Sheila Howe turns cross-cultural conflict on its head by testing the stamina of a central Asian man in a Canadian construction site in winter. "Gusts of brown dirt cast a dull dusty sheen on the landscape as particles of insulation and sawdust swirled in the relentless wind." The final scene is astounding, showing what happens when alien techniques of survival are virtually parachuted into Canadian conditions.

The character Pancho, invented by Angelo Eidse in his story "Pancho and Gary," is arguably one of the most powerful in cross-cultural literature. When he and old-fashioned, Anglo-Saxon discipline come face-to-face, the sparks fly; how the conflict is resolved will amaze you.

James Romanow's "The Mangohattan" places two white ex-Winnipeggers in exotic Bombay in his economical, fast-paced style. "You are too conservative. You never were open to experience." That remark reflects another far deeper difference that drives this richly layered story of rejection and survival, benevolence and antagonism: "'Oh where is the tender heart that I remember' . . . When she said those words I knew there was no going back. Janet had become Indian."

"Inca'sReturn" by the poet Cyril Dabydeen presents disturbing images of the North (Canada) and the South (anywhere very hot), emotional metaphors for the stark opposition of cultures, and the interdependence of the human and the natural. He brings to life the relationship between spirituality and the natural world, where the boundaries between the boy Inca and nature are indivisible or invisible. "Inca wanted the old images of palm trees, mango, star apple to remain with him forever, as a humming noise he heard deep in his brain." The power of place illuminates Dabydeen's world.

Co-editor Radhika Sekar's "Swearing at the Queen" rounds off the collection with a delightful romp through political correctness and prejudice. Sandwiched in the courtroom in which landed immigrants are legally transformed into Canadian citizens, the characters' private thoughts and reactions to each other yield cynical—and deadly accurate— gems of hilarious comment on what it means to be Canadian. The final line will stun you.

This book marks the appearance, perhaps for the first time ever, of a short story collection focused solely on the cross-cultural nature of Canadian society. It is the result of a richly productive nation-wide cross-cultural contest, part of Canada's "literary renaissance underway" (Kirkus Review).

Students, educators, political officials, public servants, and researchers will be interested in the knowledge the book offers on the contemporary scene. This is because it relates directly to areas such, as Canadian Studies, psychology, religion, sociology, cultural/social anthropology, Canadian Literature, geopolitics, government policy and programs—any field in which cultural matters are key.

For example, the increasing cultural plurality of Canadian society and literature has brought new vantages to bear on the developing world—a dispersed geo-world existing partly right here at home, in our North. Our authors depict this world both inside and outside of Canada. They show how we in the globalized world have failed to come to terms with the impact of the developing world on our lives. Following the image provided by author James Romanow, they show how that world is grinding up against our consciousness, invading like an iceberg in our path, intrusive, and unavoidable. Ironically, when the point of view is reversed - you are living in, or hail from the developing world - that is exactly how it feels when the globalized world invades your life.

These stories are what brilliant short fiction should be, constantly surprising us with intense, funny, wise, and shattering characters. Our authors are not all of equal writing strength, yet their art is subtle enough to allow the reader to play a part in the creative process. Their voices have assurance as they insert recurring patterns and images like hints of the same colour in a good painting, adding texture and depth. At moments they show the sensitivity to cultural detail we find in the work of Michael Ondaatje, and Guy Vanderhaeghe.

Our stories naturally evince historical Canadian literary themes like survival, geographical and/or emotional isolation, and helplessness in the face of evil. Margaret Atwood said in Survival (1972) that our literature is preoccupied with victims, day-to-day life in an inhospitable, often dangerous environment, Canada. She saw survival, not so much as conquering a frontier, an obstacle or an enemy, but as enduring, coming out unscathed. In fact our authors go beyond the endurance theme. Their protagonists indeed struggle to conquer an obstacle to realize their dreams. The resulting tension of opposites makes for fiction that is very tough yet amazingly touching and bittersweet.

Frank Symons, PhD
Perth, Ontario

Mother Margaret and
the Rhinoceros Café
Timothy Kaiser

Mother Margaret's place was a mess. The floor, usually swept and scrubbed clean, was a marsh of sandy boot tracks and melting snow. The teapot, which had always welcomed me with a song, sat overturned beside the old cook stove. Mother Margaret's three children were knotted in an anaemic clump on the sofa, mesmerized by the cartoons on TV. I knew that if Mother Margaret had been home, Billy Jack Jr. would be up sweeping the floor like a demon. Mary Rose would be at the kitchen table bent over her math homework and Mother Margaret giving encouragement in Dene while she stitched a pair of gloves from beaver fur, or cut caribou meat into thin slices to dry on racks above the cook stove. Little Joe would be outside, bringing an axe almost as big as he down on stubborn logs.

The ritual of stopping at Mother Margaret's for a cup of tea on my way home from school had begun a few weeks after I arrived in Black Lake. I had been at home one late afternoon, trying to work through the frustration of planning my next day of classes at the Black Lake Band School, when I heard a knock at the door. I wasn't in the mood for interruptions, but my short time on the reserve had taught me that everyone seemed to always know where I was and

11

pretending I wasn't home would only lead to embarrassing questions later on. Whoever was knocking knew that I was home. So I trotted to the door in the hope that the pencil gripped between my teeth and the notebook rolled in my hand would serve as a strong enough deterrent or excuse.

Given the boisterous, persistent knocking, I was surprised to open the door on a girl of no more than five or six. Her arms were crossed in an expression of disapproval and impatience as she leaned back in her boots to look me over. She was about to speak but was distracted by noises behind her. I peered out the door to where the girl had turned her attention and saw several other children about her age arranged acrobatically around the lower railing of my stairs. They were giggling and pointing at me, and at the little girl. Good, I thought—kids. Much easier to get rid of. I was just about to herd them away when the girl who had done the knocking started berating her companions in Dene. Then she turned back abruptly to me and said, "You come now. Mother Margaret wanna talk to you."

I thought desperately about the lessons I had yet to plan, about the mossy dishes piled precariously high in the sink, about the letter home I was finally hoping to have time to write about this unusual place I had somehow found myself in, but there was something in the girl's tone which led me to believe that a meeting with Mother Margaret, whoever she might be, was unavoidable, if not urgent. So I put the notebook and pencil down, locked the door behind me, and marched after my brigade of kindergarten guides, some of whom had already disappeared over the surprisingly Sahara-like dunes bordering the lake.

As I caught up, I fell into step with the girl who seemed to be the spokesperson. I asked her a few questions about Mother Margaret, but she continued on in silence. I asked her companions the same questions, but they seemed intent on one thing only: dislodging dead branches from the scrub brush pimpled around the reserve, which they hurled as spears at automobile carcasses along our path. After awhile, the children dropped the branches in favour of stones, which they aimed at yawning, unhurried dogs, far out of range. I knew after a short while that whatever Mother Margaret wanted me for, it certainly wasn't urgent.

We came finally to a small house halfway up the hill from the school to the Black Lake Band Hall. I had noticed the house before because of its brilliant purple with pink trim. Against the indigo backdrop of the lake and the tawny stretches of sand on which the reserve was built, and amongst the odd bush which the kids that day seemed bent on obliterating, the colourful house always looked like an unfound Easter egg as I descended the hill on my way home from school. My platoon halted and pointed. Standing in the doorway, with a dishtowel slung over her shoulder, was a woman. As soon as she saw me, she backed into the purple porch and disappeared.

I wasn't sure what to do next. Had we, after four direct hits on an old Ford and a barrage that threatened to collapse a spidery outhouse, finally arrived at Mother Margaret's house? Had that been Mother Margaret in the doorway? I turned to the group of kids to ask, but they had already scattered. The little girl who had uttered the strange summons —"You come now. Mother Margaret wanna talk to you"—was heading away, cheerfully dragging her feet through the sand, splashing backwards through

13

my own footprints on her way down the hill. Feeling now as though I might be the butt of some elaborate prank—elaborate at least for six-year-olds—and regretting more and more the sloppy dishes back home in the sink, the uncorrected notebooks beside the sink, the blank pieces of paper beside the uncorrected notebooks which were to become a letter home detailing bizarre episodes in this community —was this another of them?—I strode purposefully into the cramped porch, piled high with split wood for the winter, and knocked at the door. No response. Come on, come on, let's get this "Mother Margaret wanna talk to you" nonsense over and done with. I leaned towards the door, listening, but the only sound I could hear was staticky country and western music. Impatient over lost time, annoyed at being the entertainment of the day, irked at having the strain and silence filled by country and western, I did not knock again. I pounded. And this time a gruff voice called out above the crackly chords, "Take your boots off."

What choice, for the second time in one day, did a commanding voice leave me? I leaned over and slowly pulled off my boots. Not so much in a hurry now, I realised that I was about to enter a splendid purple and pink house—a poster home for bargain-bin paint warehouses, a house possibly belonging to a mysterious Mother Margaret, who, according to an informant not higher than my waist, had something she wished to discuss with me. And I would be entering minus my boots, thereby making a hasty retreat should things go bad, as they appeared likely to do, completely out of the question. Just don't look scared, I thought, as I stepped out of the porch and through the front door. Look confident, I thought, as I gazed down at my floppy wool socks with holes in the toes, tagged with sawdust spikes from the porch. And inside that bucket in the porch beside which I had placed my boots—was that blood?

As I stepped out of the porch with its wood chips and possible evidence of criminal wrongdoing, I entered the kitchen and there by the cook stove sat the woman I had just seen. She was folding laundry and humming along to an old radio, which sat half-buried under a pile of rumpled clothes. Without looking up from her work, the woman said in that same gruff tone I felt I had already heard once too often that day, "Siddown. Have some tea."

I didn't want to sit down. The command initially given by a semi-mute dwarf, this incongruous house —possibly the site of God only knew what atrocity— this second invitation of the day delivered by an un-friendly, possibly homicidal woman, made me want my boots back on, my footprints in the sand headed, with very long strides, down the hill, my lessons planned, my dishes washed, and my letter started with "Just when I thought I had experienced it all...." Seeing me hesitate, the woman spoke again, "Sid-down. Have some tea and some caribou jerky." In a bucket beside the table was a lump of raw meat, and on the table were meat slices, thinly cocooned in blood, neatly arranged in rows. Ah, could that ex-plain the blood in the bucket in the porch? Breathing a shallow sigh of relief, I shuffled over to the table with my socks slapping much too loudly on the floor. Even though the ounce of confidence I thought I had mustered when entering was gone, I knew I would have to stay focussed and find out immedi-ately what this mysterious Mother Margaret, if in-deed the woman I was facing was Mother Margaret, wanted from me. I moved over to a chair, picked up a pile of clothes lying there, and expected to be told

15

where to put it. I wasn't. The woman studied me for a moment, then asked, "Like country music?" I squeezed out a nervous lie and watched to see how convincing I had been.

"ME, I LOOOOOOVE COUNTRY MUSIC!!!!!" Unsettled as I had been for a considerable length of time, the woman's exuberant response startled me and I fumbled most of the laundry I had been holding onto the floor. As I bent down to pick it up, I heard the woman laugh. It was a deep, warm laugh and when it gave way once again to the slow, staticky rhythms on the radio, I felt strangely at ease. "Name's Margaret Bouvier," she said as she reached to pour me a cup of tea, "Everybody 'round here calls me Mother Margaret... but I ain't no nun, that's for sure." This set off another round of laughter, and I watched as the ripples of delight spread until they made small waves of Margaret's whole body. I suddenly realized that I had never met anyone in my entire life who could laugh like that. She seemed to be able to make her whole kitchen, and everything in it, including me, as I would discover more over time, vibrate to the rhythm of her own joy.

After she stopped laughing, Mother Margaret leaned forward suddenly, unslung the towel from around her shoulders and began wiping the table nervously. I watched her closely, the pit in my stomach returning as I realised that I still had no clue why Mother Margaret had asked for me to come in the first place. "Teacher, I got a problem," she said with a touch of sadness, "My boy, Billy Jack Jr., he's in school now and he brings home sometimes those books he wants me to read for him." I had to wait several moments before she continued, "But you know, Teacher, I was raised mostly in the bush. Dad and mom had a trapline and all us kids helped out the winter. I never seen most a those words Billy Jack Jr. brought home before."

I discovered that the word that was giving Mother Margaret trouble that day appeared in the title of a book which her son had brought home from the school library. She knew he would ask her to read it to him later that night and she was embarrassed that she couldn't even read the title. The book was called Jake Meets a Rhinoceros. I pronounced "rhinoceros" for her, and Mother Margaret's belly shook a few more times before she was finally able to repeat it to her satisfaction. She laughed even harder when she told me how surprised Billy Jack Jr. would be to find out his mother was finally smarter than he. Before I left that day—home to my dishes and notebooks and neglected letters which had somehow become less important—I had one nagging unresolved question for Mother Margaret: "Why me? I mean, there are at least 15 teachers at the Band School, so why did you send your midget posse after me?"

Mother Margaret's response was quick and lively, delivered with a wink, "You know, Teacher, when you walk home from school, sometimes you whistle. It don't sound very good, but it's cute. I'm not sayin' that you're cute... your whistlin' is."

After that first visit, I often went to Mother Margaret's house. I never waited for another invitation. It never seemed that I needed one. I always looked forward to my visits with her, especially on days when I felt the loneliness and interminability of the northern winter and the confusion of living in a community so different from any I had ever known. Mother Margaret would be sitting there at her table surrounded by piles of laundry, or bloody caribou meat, or books. The transistor radio would always be on, and she would be sometimes singing, sometimes just humming along with her country and western idols. She told me often how her "all-star favourite singer" was Crystal Gale, "even though most people don't even know who she is anymore." She said that Crystal Gale "sang like an angel and was more beautiful than one with that long, black hair like a raven." Margaret told me that she herself had won second prize in the previous year's Black Lake Winter Carnival for her rendition of Crystal Gale's "Ready for the Times to Get Better." After that, Margaret said, people in Black Lake sometimes called her the Chipewyan Queen of Nashville, just to tease her.

It was always hard for me to picture Margaret on stage, performing to a packed house at the band hall. In fact, it was hard for me to picture her anywhere outside her home, away from her kitchen table, ordering her kids around as she stirred stew or stitched moccasins. That's what made that visit so unusual the day I walked into Mother Margaret's home and she wasn't there. I couldn't imagine why she would have left her house long enough that her kids were able to turn it into a totally uncharacteristic scene of disorder and apathy.

I asked Billy Jack Jr. where his mother was and he motioned listlessly, without taking his eyes off the TV screen, "At the band store down by the lake."

The band store was an old, graffiti-riddled steel Quonset that I always passed on my way to school. Many times as I passed, I read the weathered sign above the door, "Black Lake Band Store—Welcome Friends." The two caribou silhouettes that bordered the sign were chewed through by bullet holes. The store itself had been the product of a dispute between band members and the Hudson's Bay Company store over alleged over-pricing. The band council, in an effort to break the Bay's monopoly, had built the store, stocked the shelves, and hired a manager. The first manager left after only one month with all of the store's first cash receipts. The second manager was related to everyone on the reserve and he had a hard time taking money from relatives. After he had given away almost everything in the store, the band council put a padlock on the door, and told everyone to go back to the Bay.

I could see that the padlock was off the store as I approached. I pushed the door open and heard the soft, slow rhythms of a female country and western singer coming from somewhere inside. I peered into the darkness. Eerie red and green flashes of light came from what looked like an old-style jukebox. "Margaret, are you in there, Margaret?" I called out.

"Zat you, Teacher? C'mon in if your boots are clean."

The large figure of Margaret entered into the beam of light cast through the open door.

"Wanna dance? I dragged that old piece a junk outta the back room."

Her face was beaded with sweat and she kept flicking a stray piece of hair back behind her ear. She used the towel from her shoulder to wipe the sweat from her forehead while I spoke.

"Billy Jack Jr. told me you were here, but I thought I must have gotten the message wrong." I looked around the abandoned store, my eyes gradually becoming accustomed to the dark. "What are you doing here, anyway?"

Mother Margaret motioned to two chairs and I was beginning to make out a few more chairs and tables arranged in a neat pattern.

"How ya like it?" she began.

"Like what?"

"The restaurant. Gettin' the power all checked out tomorrow. Got the chairs and tables all set up, hamburger patties on the way by cargo plane from P.A., and a new grill's all set and ready to go. I'm a businesswoman now, Teacher, so you better not mess with me."

Margaret went on to tell me that she had approached the band council for permission to open the old store as a restaurant. They had obliged, quite happily as it turned out, since the current chief had been involved in the opening of the store in the first place and was tired of answering questions about its demise. It was agreed that Margaret would rent the store for $100 a month and she could do whatever she wanted with it.

"I got tired a pickin' up that government cheque every month," Margaret explained. "Just figured there had to be more to it... Besides, my old man, he don't help any to pay the bills."

It wasn't the first time Margaret had mentioned problems with her husband. Billy Jack Bouvier had a good-paying job at a uranium mine in the south and came back to Black Lake only occasionally. When he did come back, it was always, as Mother Margaret described it, "to drink and party and mess around where he gots no business." Mother Margaret was always relieved when he got on the plane to fly south.

"Us Indian women we gotta learn to take care a ourselves," Margaret continued. "Nobody else's gonna do it for us." She picked up a ketchup bottle and dusted it off. I looked around the room again and picked out other shapes—old grocery shelves pushed into the corners to make room for tables and chairs, tablecloths on the tables, napkin holders on the tablecloths. I could even make out more precisely the silhouette of Mother Margaret, her body swaying in time to the slow, soft music from the jukebox.

Within a few days, as Mother Margaret had said, the power was on and the grill was installed. Mother Margaret asked me to help her with a few posters she was planning to put up around town to advertise her new enterprise. The name she had chosen for the restaurant was "The Rhinoceros Café." She liked the sound of it, she said, especially when it came out of her own mouth. "Besides," she said to me with a grin, "that rhinoceros reminds me of me—fat, slow, and just barely survivin'."

In spite of the fact that everyone on the reserve seemed to know what was going on before the first poster even went up, Mother Margaret insisted that we staple her posters to the bulletin boards in the store, the band hall, the band office, and the clinic. She seemed to get a special thrill from reading out loud the information on each poster after she tacked it up. She had traced a rhinoceros from Billy Jack Jr.'s library book and coloured it with a gray crayon. The caption at the top read: "Mother Margaret's Rhinoceros Cafe, best dam food in the north."

On a snowy Friday afternoon in January, Mother Margaret's Rhinoceros Café officially opened. I stopped by on my way home from school. I had hoped to be the first customer, but there were a few who had arrived before me. Margaret was busy behind the counter, but she looked up and smiled a greeting. "What can I get you, Teacher? Special today's caribou brain on toast." Then she laughed her unforgettable laugh as she wiped the sweat from her forehead. "Billy Jack Jr., go get Teacher a cup a coffee. He looks like he had a rough day."

As I drank my coffee, I glanced around to see how the place looked. The few customers who had arrived earlier were mostly band elders. They were huddled around a cribbage board, counting their points in Dene through missing teeth. The tables were covered with red and white checkered tablecloths, a few of the corners dragging on the floor. There were silk flowers in vases on each table. On one of the stems I spotted the price tag which had not yet been removed. In the corner sat the jukebox wheezing out another mournful country and western ballad. Mother Margaret was squeezing down a sizzling hamburger patty on the grill. Huge, black kettles gurgled beside her. On the floor near the grill sat six ten-gallon pails of water which Mother Margaret and Billy Jack Jr. had carried to the restaurant that morning before school. On the wall above where Margaret worked, she had posted the café's prices. A "hambugger" was $3.50 and a "cup a cofee - 75sents." At the bottom of the price list, Margaret had again drawn a rhinoceros—this one wearing sunglasses and a cowboy hat.

I started spending more and more time in the Rhinoceros Café after it opened. I was lonely and the realisation had slowly dawned on me that it didn't help to barricade myself in my house planning lessons that rarely turned out the way they were intended or writing letters trying to describe things that were rarely as they seemed. "Teacher," Mother Margaret liked to tease me, "you get yourself a nice Indian wife so you got some reason to stay home."

In the next few weeks, business picked up and the Rhinoceros Cafe was usually full: Mother Margaret seldom moved from behind the counter. Her kids scurried around her, holding plates that she would pile high with fries and cheeseburgers. Then she would pat their behinds in a mock gesture of impatience as they wobbled off to deliver the order to a waiting customer. She did the two-step as she moved from the wash basin to the grill. She made loud, thunderous wisecracks in Dene over her shoulder to her customers. She never stopped smiling.

One night, a few weeks after the restaurant opened, I had a knock on the door. It was the same girl who had come the day I first met Mother Margaret. And she issued the same summons. "You come now. Mother Margaret wanna talk to you."

I hadn't visited Mother Margaret at home since the restaurant opened. I thought it strange that she would be there since the Rhinoceros Café didn't normally close for another few hours. She was sitting alone when I walked in, her elbow on the table and her head in her hand. She managed a weak smile as I approached.

"What's the matter, Margaret?" I asked, struggling to mask my alarm. She motioned for me to sit down.

"Just a little tired, that's all... Closed up early tonight... Nothin' much." She turned to me and a search of her eyes told me that there was more. "Chief he come and talked to me today. He said some people say I gotta pay more rent money. They're sayin' like $400 a month... I don't care. The cafe's doin' good. I'll pay, if that's what they want." After a long silence, Mother Margaret began again. Her next words were much more painful. "The chief he also said some people say I work my kids too hard down at the Rhinoceros. That I don't take good care a them and they're doin' bad in school now they're workin' every day."

A tear started down Mother Margaret's cheek, which she quickly brushed away. "Like I told you before, Teacher, I was raised in the bush. We had to work hard to survive. That's what I want my kids to learn. I don't want them all day playin' video games down at the store, or sniffin' out behind the clinic. I love my kids. Just wanna be proud a them and make them good."

Mother Margaret hugged her large arms tight to herself and waited for my reply. I wasn't sure how to start. "Margaret," I began slowly, measuring how to make it sound as reassuring as I so desperately wanted it to sound. "I wouldn't worry about how your kids are doing in school; I know all of their teachers and I've never heard a single bad report— before and especially not now that the restaurant has opened. As far as what people will say, I guess there's talk like that in every town."

Mother Margaret exhaled in a faint whistle. "I don't know why people gotta go messin' around in other people's business. I got a nice restaurant, a nice family, and a nice purple and pink house. They're just jealous, that's all." She laughed after she said this, but not as loud as I had hoped.

Throughout the winter, Margaret made improvements to the Rhinoceros Cafe when she could. She painted the walls and extended the counter so more customers could be closer to where she worked. The most significant addition, however, was the stereo system she ordered from an electronics store in P.A. The old jukebox had long been a headache for Margaret. She adored the dancing lights and the hissing sound it made while selections were changing, but it was old and temperamental. Margaret couldn't stand it when the machine stopped in the middle of a song or skipped to another.

So she ordered a new stereo to replace the juke-box. It was an expensive stereo. In fact, Margaret had looked through the store's catalogue and selected one of the most expensive ones she could find. "If Crystal Gale's gonna sing like an angel in the Rhinoceros Cafe," Mother Margaret reasoned, "I better get her some damn good wings."

I helped Margaret set up the stereo one Saturday morning as we hurried to get it ready to greet the lunch crowd already trickling in. Emma Big Bear was the first to comment on the stereo. When she walked in and saw Margaret and me fiddling with the wires from behind the speakers, she mumbled under her breath, "What's that Margaret up to now? No one else in Black Lake's got a stereo like that." Then Emma walked out, without another word. Mervin Sandypoint was on his way in when Emma pushed through the door. She mumbled something to him as she passed by. Mervin stared at us for a few moments as he kicked snow off his boots. Then he too disappeared out the door.

The rest of the afternoon was much the same. People came in, looked over the stereo, and walked out. Finally, no one came anymore except a few elders who entered quietly and sat in a corner with a crib board.

Before Emma Big Bear had come in, Mother Margaret couldn't contain her excitement as we unwrapped and unravelled the stereo components from their boxes. Throughout the afternoon, however, her mood changed noticeably. She didn't express to me in words how she was feeling, but I could tell from the unusual heaviness of her motions how troubled she was. When we got all the wires of the stereo connected, she didn't even want to turn it on. She poured herself a cup of coffee and slumped down behind the counter. "I shoulda known...," she said finally. "It's sometimes tough on the reserve, Teacher. You grow up with these people. Most of them are related to you. But the important difference is sometimes they're friends. Sometimes they're not." I tried to reassure Margaret that soon everyone would forget about the stereo and everything would return to normal. She looked hopeful for a moment, then her eyes filled with sadness. She spoke her next words so softly I could hardly hear them. "No... it's over, Teacher. I could keep goin', but I got no go left. You don't know what people say behind my back. First, I was the crazy Indian wanted to start a res- taurant. Then, I was the bad mother didn't look after her kids. Then I was the cheatin' wife foolin' round with a white teacher..." She paused as she said this but not long enough for me to protest. "Today, I'm the rich woman too good for everyone else. There's always my regulars, and I guess you're right— people forget.... But tonight when I lock up, that's the end of the trail for Mother Margaret and the Rhinoceros Café."

The next morning I saw that there were no ski- doos parked in front of the Rhinoceros Café. The old padlock was back on the door and a fresh dusting of snow had covered tracks from the night before. I walked up to Mother Margaret's purple and pink house, knocked on the door, took my boots off, and entered. She had her new stereo set on an old bench beside the cook stove. Already it was piled high with clothes.

Mother Margaret was singing loudly when I came in. She winked at me and motioned to pull up a chair. Her spirits seemed to have returned as I watched her sashay around her kitchen. "Teacher," she said as she turned the volume down, "Just thinkin' last night after I got home that I should start up a country and western band. We could go all over the North on our ski-doos and play concerts in band halls. We could write our own songs in Dene. We'll take you along and you can whistle in the background." And then Mother Margaret laughed. The cook stove popped and crackled. The teakettle sang. The stereo played on.

Incident on 33
James Romanow

The elevator doors opened on eleven, and for a moment Rasheed was incapable of getting off. He took a deep breath and started walking. As he entered the office, everyone grew silent. Eyes swivelled, looked at him, then refocused on work. An artificial hum of chatter rose up, filling the silence, denying anything was different.

He picked his way through the desks, heading toward Sharkey's office. Some co-workers mumbled greetings: mostly variations of "How ya doin'." But two managed to look right at him and say, "Good luck."

Sharkey watched Rasheed's progress through the plate glass that formed the wall between his office and his department. If it wasn't one damn thing it was another, he thought. He could feel his stomach souring, in anticipation of the coming interview.

Rasheed stopped on the threshold of the office.

"Shut the door," Sharkey said. "Sit." He glared at Rasheed for a few seconds. "You've put us in a helluva spot you know."

Us? Rasheed thought.

Sharkey continued. "Ron Kovacks called me last night. He's executive vice. He's put O'Keefe in charge of getting her side of the case."

"Her side?"

Sharkey leaned back into his chair, his mouth slightly twisted, looking at Rasheed through half-shut eyes. "Didn't expect that, did you? You figured it was all about love? Well bucko, the late breaking news is that O'Keefe gets her side, I get yours, and then O'Keefe and I press your cases to Kovacks. So . . . start talking."

"About what?"

Sharkey felt the red haze of anger intensify. "You think I need this? You think maybe there aren't more important things on my desk? I'll tell you about what. About you and whatshername and the god-damn stairwell!"

Rasheed looked over his shoulder, through the plate glass wall, to see if anyone had heard. The office was close to soundproof. But even though they knew they would hear nothing, at least a few of his co-workers were eyeing the plate glass window, watching to see his fate.

"It wasn't like that," Rasheed said. "We have been dating for some time." How was he going to explain? How could he tell Sharkey—a choleric forty-year-old, too old to remember love—about Rajini? How could he explain the perfection that was her ear? Or the graceful arc of her neck?

Rasheed looked down at his shoes, perfectly polished, maroon brogues, shoes his grandfather would have called Sahib shoes. God knew what his grandfather would have said about his current trouble. No. That wasn't true. He would have told Rasheed that this is what comes from getting involved with an infidel. Worse, a Hindu.

Sharkey waited. When Rasheed did not elaborate, he said "For how long? When did you meet? Who

29

asked who out? If I'm going to keep your ass from a sling I need details."

"It was the Christmas party," Rasheed said.

He had leaned forward, to fill his glass from the non-alcoholic punch bowl, and had seen for the first time, her ear. Her thick glossy hair was pulled back into a heavy chignon, exposing her slender neck and the delicate nautilus spiral of her ear. It was a revelation. It felt like he was seeing, really seeing, for the first time. As if his vision were a gift from God.

"So? Did you ask her out? Or did she ask you?"

"I don't remember!" Rasheed cried. "It was mutual."

They had shared a taxi home, talking, laughing. He had seen her to the door of her apartment and she had turned and looked up at him. He knew then he would kiss her, that their lips would meet, that their tongues would bypass words for more direct communication.

But not that night.

"You didn't even kiss her?"

Rasheed knew that his story was unbelievable, especially in this city of vertiginous concrete, and taxis, and random encounters. Love, with all its reticence, did not happen here.

But it was true. He had not kissed her for three weeks. When she finally allowed it, a fuse was lit. He had been incapable of keeping his hands on her waist. She had broken away, panting, and left him, on the street outside her apartment block. This happened four times. Then one evening in February, they had gone out for a dessert and a coffee. They were seated on a low small couch, in a busy café, neither speaking. Rajini turned to him and said, "Why don't we go back to my place."

The evening was a blur from that moment. He remembered throwing a bill on the table, far too much for the little they had eaten, and walking a few short blocks to her apartment. He was unable to keep his hands off her, even for that brief distance. They were barely inside the door when she turned to him, pressing her mouth to his. They did not make it to the bedroom. He had pulled her clothes off there in the foyer, and they made love on the floor.

It was unbelievable.

It was also an isolated incident.

She lived with her mother.

Their first encounter had been an enormous stroke of luck. Her mother had gone back briefly to India to settle a family matter. She returned in less than a week.

They had survived, living for afternoon encounters at his apartment on weekends, supplemented by brief fumbles on her doorstep. It had driven him crazy. He had pushed her. He had wanted more. She protested when he tried to get her to stay over at his place. "Rasheed, I cannot. They would disown me." That was where it all went wrong.

"It was my fault," Rasheed said. "I put the idea in her head."

"What idea?" Sharkey asked.

They had been lying amidst the wreckage of the bedding, in his bedroom. He had asked if he could see her during the week.

"Rasheed I can't," she said. "I must be home by ten. Any later, and she is suspicious. She looks at my underwear when she does the laundry."

"So?" he said. "Don't wear any." And then, with a smile, he had leaned over, brushing the purple-black cone of her nipple with one hand as he pressed his mouth to her throat. He loved her perfume, a smell of cedar and spice and something indefinable. A smell that was perfect.

He had been lucky. Work got busy after that, giving him no time to worry about their problem. But she had found a way to burst through his preoccupation.

It was in the company restaurant—really nothing more than an upscale cafeteria—she had smiled at him across the table they shared. "Notice anything different?" she asked.

He had not. The bond issue had been taking up all of his time for the last few days. He had only managed to send her a single e-mail.

She smiled across that white industrial table, across the beige plastic of her food tray, filled as usual with yoghurt and salad. And then she leaned forward saying "I'm not wearing any panties."

He thought he would faint. He stared into her beautiful liquid brown eyes, but his mind was filled with the thought of her belly, her thighs, and the crucial junction where they met . . . .

"Cat got your tongue?" she said. She wore a smile that he knew from school. It was the small, knowing, smirk found most famously on the Mona Lisa. She licked her spoon clean of the yoghurt. "Are you free after work?"

He had moaned then. A real moan, loud enough to cause Harrison, at an adjacent table to look over at him. "I cannot. We have a bond issue coming out. We have meetings all afternoon and into the evening . . . Later? Can I see you later?"

He knew the answer before she said no. Ten o'clock. The witching hour. When she had to be home to Mama. Her face gave away her disappointment. Then she brightened, her eyes twinkling and her smile returned. She tossed her head, moving her

32

heavy mane of perfumed hair back on her jacket. He had lost himself in that mane a few times. He remembered burying his face in it, his lips on her neck, his body arched over hers.

"You'll just have to wait then, won't you?" she said.

"And then Harrison got sick," Sharkey said. "I sent you to New York in his place." He barked a short laugh. "You didn't come back until Sunday night. You didn't see her until Monday morning."

"Lunch,"Rasheed said. "The earliest we could meet was lunch."

It had been in the cafeteria again. He had watched her walk to their table, watching every twitch of her hips. She had sat down, casually crossing her legs, her stockings rubbing against each other, her skirt riding halfway up her thigh. He could not look elsewhere, but her skirt, a tailored dark wool, gave nothing away.

"Tonight?" he asked. She tried to look amused, distant, sophisticated, like the women she saw in the movies. But he saw the truth in the slight widening of her pupils and the faintest flush gathering on her cheekbones and at the hollow of her throat. Then another emotion crossed her face, the shock of disappointment.

"I cannot!" she said. "Mother has a doctor's appointment at six. I will not be home till after seven, perhaps much later. It is impossible."

"Tomorrow?" he asked. And she nodded. She tried to smile but it didn't work. They ate little. At that moment neither cared about food. At the end of the lunch hour she stood to go. As she stood, Rasheed was aware of the hiss of her stockings as they rubbed together. She leaned down and said, "My garter belt is silk." Then, she walked away, leaving him sitting there, staring, watching her stroll toward the exit.

The next day—yesterday! Not even twenty-four hours ago! They met by chance, just before lunch, on the thirty-third floor. He was coming out of Meeting Room A, and she from Room C. They had contrived to let the others go first, to avoid crowding the elevators. Once they were alone, she reached out, grasping him by the hand, drawing him into the stairwell.

"The rest you know," Rasheed said. He lifted his head to look at Sharkey. "I would marry her tomorrow if her parents would allow it."

Sharkey shifted. He had been leaning back in his chair, as if to get some distance from Rasheed. "Yeah. Right. Well. Let's hope that cuts some ice with Kovacks."

"I'll get this typed up and e-mail it to you this afternoon. You need to sign it, or change it or whatever, and fax it back to me. Show it to a lawyer if you like. Okay?"

"Okay."

"Look, kid, don't worry. I'll work something out. Even Kovacks knows how hard it is to replace someone in this department right now. We'll get you back here in a couple of days."

Rasheed nodded. "Thanks." He did not care about work. Once it had been his greatest dream to take Sharkey's job, or go even higher than that. Now, nothing mattered. Nothing, but if he would ever see Rajini again.

On the twenty-second floor, in the same building, Heather O'Keefe arranged the table of one of the lesser boardrooms. She placed two pads on the table, and two pencils. Rajini appeared in the doorway.

"Sit down," O'Keefe said, as she closed the door. Once Rajini was sitting, O'Keefe drew a deep breath and began. "Everything said in this room goes no further. Ron Kovacks has appointed me to hear your case, and to present it to him. I need you to tell me everything. I need to understand why—," O'Keefe broke off. She did not want her anger to show. "What motivated you. We both know this is not like you. I mean, you've never acted this way before."

Rajini nodded. Never acted this way before? Well, of course not. She had not met Rasheed before.

O'Keefe smiled, trying for a sympathetic manner. Most people thought her forbidding. She was blessed with high cheekbones and blonde hair, but as she aged she looked more severe. She once had overheard a young man describing her as "a hatchet-faced old battle axe." She later fired him, doubtless reinforcing his opinion.

"Don't look so fearful. Ron knows me, and he knows your work. I don't want to lose you, and that means a great deal." Her words were not helping. Rajini was small but fear seemed to shrink her further. The thought of this slight, shy, young woman in the arms of Rasheed disturbed O'Keefe. He was a big guy, broad shouldered and more than six feet tall. He carried himself with all the arrogance you find in traders, people whose daily work is counted in millions.

"You have to tell me about what happened," O'-Keefe said. She picked up the pencil and wrote the date across the top of the first page.

Rajini looked down at her lap, her hands beneath the level of the table. "What happened?" she whispered. She looked up, and then out the window. "At Christmas," she said in a small voice. "We met at the Christmas party."

O'Keefe's face was immobile, but her left hand twitched. The party had been her doing. Her department, Strategic Planning, was too small. She had invited the traders, to add some spice to the mix. She had noticed Rasheed when he walked into the room. He was easily the best looking man there, with his exotic light brown skin, and wavy black hair. Rumour had it that he was open to all comers. She and Joan, from Internal Auditing, had joked about having some Christmas cheer with him. O'Keefe would never have thought that this quiet little woman could have pulled off what neither she nor Joan had the nerve to try.

"We shared a cab home," Rajini said. Her voice had gained a little volume and she was speaking with some authority now.

"So the affair started then," O'Keefe said, her pencil scratching across the paper.

"It wasn't what you think! It wasn't an affair!"

The pain in her voice stopped the pencil mid-word. O'Keefe looked up.

How could Rajini make this woman—this iceberg—understand? Had any man ever warmed O'-Keefe's heart? How then could Rajini explain the look in Rasheed's eye, that longing for something, for her?

She had resisted. She had tried to be a good daughter. But she had been drawn to him like a meteor to earth. They had shared a table in the cafeteria downstairs. She had gone out for coffee with him a few times, but she had not let him touch her, she had not let him kiss her. As long as there was no contact she could have resisted. But there on the steps of her apartment block, she had paused, and looked up. She had tilted her head back, and looked into his eyes. His head had ratcheted down toward her, moving incrementally as her defences melted under his gaze. She had let him press his lips to hers.

That was the mistake.

But still she resisted. She had refused him more than a kiss. She had ignored his hands as they gripped her, pulling her to him.

Then, he began sending e-mail.

O'Keefe interrupted. "This was at work? He sent you e-mails at work?" That greasy bastard! Harassment! They had him! He was toast! She made a note to have the backups of the e-mails records sent to her.

"Yes. No. I don't remember!" Rajini said. But she did remember. "No. They were sent to my private account." And every night for three more weeks, every single night, she would read those letters, off her laptop in the privacy of her bedroom, before she went to bed. Sometimes there would be two or three in a single day. They were passionate letters, telling her of his desire to press his lips to hers, to taste her lips, her breasts, her belly.

"Did he send you flowers too? Was there any other kind of pressure?"

Pressure! What pressure was needed?

Then it seemed as if the very gods were conspiring her fall. Her mother was called home. But still she resisted. She was good for two days and two nights without her mother.

She remembered sitting in the loud, trendy, restaurant, sipping a cappuccino, their knees touching. She looked across her cup at him. Their eyes met. And there, on that tacky blue love seat, in a raucous café, Rajini knew she would resist no longer. She could feel her heart beating, the blood rushing through her. She had not been able to speak. Her eyes had been enough of an invitation.

Rasheed had stood, throwing two twenties on the table, and held out his hand to her. They were just around the corner from the apartment. They had walked back in silence, but Rasheed's left hand was on her buttock, his fingers and thumb caressing, following the cleft down and circling across the top of her thigh. His hands drawn to her, by the gravity of desire.

She remembered turning to him the second they crossed the threshold. She remembered sucking greedily at his mouth, his tongue. Her! The good girl! She had been unable to contain herself, and her passion had inflamed Rasheed. He had not even been able to delay long enough to make it to the bedroom.

O'Keefe stopped writing. She sat, listening to the passion pour out of the slight young woman, across the table from her. Rajini stopped speaking, and turned to look directly at O'Keefe, for the first time since she had begun. "My parents want me to marry a boy back in India," she said. Her father had returned home, accepting a post at a Mumbai University. He regularly scanned the ranks of his students seeking a good boy, a Brahmin with fine prospects, a suitable husband for his daughter.

Her mother returned. From then on they had only been able to go for coffee. There were two weeks of nothing more than kisses. But such kisses! These were kisses that Rajini knew poor O'Keefe had never known. She felt a pang of compassion for the older woman. Now, old as she was, she would never know them. Rajini brushed her hair back off her shoulder, her fingers tracing the invisible scar his lips had burnt across her neck.

"He needed more. He was going crazy. I was afraid I would lose him," she said.

He pressured her for sex. O'Keefe wrote on her pad.

She went to his apartment. She had told her mother she was going shopping. It was a Saturday morning. She was barely inside his apartment before they were tearing at their clothes, re-enacting their first encounter.

It was so easy they had repeated it the next weekend. But then her mother became suspicious.

"She knew. She could tell," Rajini said. "She would look at me, and the disappointment was in her eyes."

She had refused to meet Rasheed for another two weeks. Then he had sent her an e-mail, pouring out his soul. He missed her, he needed her. He could not sleep. He was distracted at work by the thought of her. He remembered the taste of her, and wanted more.

Then, there was silence.

She had been strong in the face of his needs, but the silence had broken her. They met for lunch, but his work kept them apart.

Then, she was coming out of a meeting on the thirty-third floor, and there he was. She looked into his eyes and saw the longing. When her hand brushed his, as they waited for the elevator, she could feel the need she provoked.

"He said we need to talk. I told him not here, not where anyone could see us. And he grabbed my hand and dragged me into the stairwell."

In the stairwell he had kissed her, and she remembered. She remembered his apartment. She remembered the feel of his lips, the weight of his body on hers. His hands cupped under her buttocks lifting her up till her face was level with his.

"I should have stopped then," she said. But she hadn't. She had leaned back, bracing her shoulders against the wall and ridden him like a jockey, clutching his ribs with her knees, his hips for stirrups.

It was over in a few breathless seconds. He hugged her to his chest panting. She wrapped her arms around his neck and hitched herself up, releasing him. "And I looked over his shoulder and there was Miss McDonald," she said. McDonald had been standing on the landing, a half floor below them, staring up, her mouth hanging open, her pale face blotched with pink.

Rajini never felt such shame.

A few seconds later, they heard the door of the floor below open and close.

O'Keefe looked up from her writing. "It was McDonald who caught you," she said. "Too bad. Anyone else, and I doubt it even would have been reported."

O'Keefe wrote a few more words on her pad. "I don't think there will be any problems from what you have told me. I'll get a copy of your statement to you, and you'll have to sign it and get it back." She looked at the younger woman, hunched in her chair. "Are you going to be okay? How is your mother taking this?"

Rajini looked out the window. There was no way to explain to O'Keefe what awaited her at home. This was her punishment. Not coming to work, not being able to escape from her mother's anger and despair. "I'll be okay," she said. "What will happen to Rasheed? He won't be . . . ."

O'Keefe stood up. "It isn't up to me. Don't worry. He'll land on his feet. His kind always does."

"I expect Ron will see me before the week is out. So see to it that you get that statement signed and back to me as soon as possible."

Two days later, late Friday afternoon, the elevator opened on thirty-three. O'Keefe stepped out and glanced around the lobby area. Nothing was changed. It was a floor O'Keefe knew well, as it was entirely dedicated to meeting rooms. She strode forward, her heels clicking on the polished granite, toward Meeting Room B. She did not even glance at the steel door to the stairwell as she walked by. It was unlikely that passion would mark the bare concrete and steel of the fire escape.

Sharkey was already seated when she entered. He lifted himself slightly out of his chair. "Heather," he said by way of greeting.

"Harold," she said, seating herself, and arranging her papers.

The silence was colder than usual.

"So," Sharkey said. "Your girl got another job yet?"

"She is neither a girl nor mine," O'Keefe said. She knew Sharkey was baiting her. "She has no need to. It's a clear case of harassment."

"Harassment? How do you figure that?" Sharkey asked.

"Come on! He's a man, and she's a vulnerable woman of colour from another culture. He earns ten times what she does, and she's vulnerable to intimidation."

"Excuse me? She works in Strategy. That makes her at least two full grades higher than Rasheed. And we both know that traders never make it into the executive suite."

They both also knew that Sharkey had reached his peak in the organization, a mere manager of the trading floor. And they both knew that his salary was based on the wages of the traders, which meant he earned several times what O'Keefe, a vice president made.

O'Keefe said, "If you kept tighter rein on your cowboys none of this would ever have happened."

"To paraphrase you, they aren't cowboys and they aren't mine."

Neither spoke again.

Kovacks came in several minutes later. "Harold, Heather. Sorry I'm late. Now then. I think the two of you have been waiting long enough. Our decision is that both will be terminated. For cause."

"What!" yelped Sharkey.

"That's impossible!" O'Keefe said.

"I'm sure you both remember John's memo of last October fourteenth. It clearly states that there will be no dating between employees. There were no exceptions."

"We'll never get another woman of colour this qualified . . . "

"Traders are impossible to find now!" Sharkey yelled over her.

"None of that matters," Kovacks cut in. "And if it makes you feel any better, I've lost the best executive secretary in the organization. Miss McDonald has been out on stress leave since she found those two rutting like animals in the stairwell."

"You can't do this, Ron. Rajini is a complete victim here. That cowboy practically raped her. He's ruined her chances of a good marriage. He's ruined her life!"

"Victim! He wants to marry her!" Sharkey yelled. "And what kind of victim comes to work and tells her boyfriend she isn't wearing panties?"

42

Kovacks walked out of the room holding up one hand, as if to ward off the yelling. He paused at the doorway. "None of any of this matters. They were both high enough up to understand the rules. They both got the memo. They both admitted they got it when Legal called them earlier today. They're fired." The door clicked shut, leaving the two managers staring at the spot where Kovacks had stood a moment earlier.

O'Keefe turned to the table, keeping her eyes from Sharkey. She gathered her memos, with short, sharp gestures.

Sharkey fell into his chair. "Shit," he said. "You know what this really is about?"

"What, Harold? Tell me what this really is about."

"It's about that goddamn ice-maiden McDonald. She wanted early retirement. She's got it, and Kovacks is pissed off at losing her."

O'Keefe snorted. "He hasn't lost her. She's holding a gun to his head."

"Gun?"

"You traders! You're all alike. Don't you ever listen to anything? Don't you know what's been going on? She hasn't retired. She's been appointed to the Ethics in Business Commission!"

"Jesus! Really? How'd she get that?"

"Really." O'Keefe's voice was hard enough to cut glass. "She goes to the same damn pickle-up-the-ass church the Premier does."

"Shit." Sharkey considered this news. "She's been here forever. She's seen every memo that crossed Kovacks' desk."

"Exactly. She's in a position to leak every single misdemeanour from the last forty years."

Sharkey shook his head. "And the price of her silence was firing those two kids. What a bitch. All they did was fall for each other." He leaned back into his chair and ran a hand over his head. "Is it true what you said? That she won't get a good marriage now?"

O'Keefe looked at Harold. He was sprawled back in the chair, his shirt rumpled, a slight paunch showing, his hair receding. He was no Rasheed. "Yes. It's true. I'd bet she was a virgin before that ape got her. From what I hear of the Hindu community, no virginity, no marriage."

"He's no ape, Heather. And her virginity won't bother him. He wants to marry her." Sharkey was silent for a moment. "You know I hate to lose him. He was a great trader. But maybe this is all for the best. Maybe now, her parents will let them marry."

His last comment made O'Keefe pause. She shook her head. "Sometimes, Harry you surprise me. You. A romantic." She picked up her papers and her pen. "Well that's it folks. God I need a drink after that one."

"You and me both. How about stopping at Bardi's for a quick one?"

She looked at him, and wondered. Her and Harry, King of the Cowboys? Nah! They were both too old for that kind of thing. Best she go home, and . . . And what? Water the cactus? The thought of the empty condo tipped the balance. "Why not? Just let me drop by my office for a minute."

He smiled at her, stood up, and walked to the door. "Let me get that," he said pulling it open.

O'Keefe snorted. "You. A romantic," she said again. But she smiled as she walked out.

Crazy
Rosemary McCracken

"Kamal!"
Not him. Kamal cursed silently and spilled a pile of salt on the sidewalk of the shopping plaza. Tightening his grip on the bag, he kept his eyes on the salt crystals he was spreading into arcs on the icy concrete.

"How you been, Kamal? Long time since I seeing you."

Kamal glanced up. Pawel had a big, goofy grin on his face. As always.

"Okay," Kamal muttered, wishing he could disappear. He thought he'd shaken Pawel when he'd left the garden centre in September. What was he doing in this part of Toronto anyway?

"Me, I come to this part of city one month ago. Got job not far away. Girlfriend and me, we renting nice apartment. Just other side of 401 highway."

Terrific, Kamal thought. He'd be bumping into Pawel all the time.

"Hey, we going for drink, Kamal. Past nine now. You must be finish soon. We having drink and talking about old times, eh?"

"Late. Must get home."

"Come on, Kamal. We having drink. Just small one."

Kamal locked up the maintenance room behind Centennial Bakery and considered heading for home through the streets behind the plaza. But Pawel knew where he worked. It would be easier to have a coffee with him, get away as soon as he could and, hopefully, that would be the end of him.

Pawel was waiting in front of the shopping plaza and led Kamal across the street. They entered a doorway under a yellow sign with the words "Restaurant Bar" in black letters. Inside, the air was warm and smokey. Kamal blinked. He was standing in a small vestibule connecting two rooms. The one to his right was filled with tables with blue-checked cloths; about half the tables were occupied. Pawel took the left doorway into a dimly lit room. A woman's voice poured out of speakers set high on a side wall. A sad, caressing voice accompanied by a tinkle of piano keys. A song about being crazy.

Pawel pulled a chair out from a corner table. "Sit, Kamal. We having drink."

Kamal sat down, keeping on his ski jacket. He looked around the room nervously.

"Some place, eh?" Pawel said, leaning back in his chair. "Come here past Saturday with Jola."

"Jola?"

"Girlfriend. Live music here Saturday night."

"Yeah?"

A waitress appeared at their table. She was wearing a short, red skirt and a black sweater. Kamal took a quick look at the cleavage displayed by the sweater's low neckline. "What are you guys havin'?" she asked, flicking back her mane of chestnut hair.

"Golden," Pawel said. "That okay, Kamal?"

Kamal had no idea what Golden was. "I not ..."

"My treat, Kamal. I buying you drink."

"Two Molson Goldens coming right up," the waitress said.

Kamal turned to her. "That song," he said, taking another look at her white breasts and neck. "What that song?"

"On the jukebox? That's an oldie. Patsy Cline singing "Crazy.""

Kamal wondered if he should know who Patsy Cline was. There was still so much he had to learn about North America.

"So, how you being, Kamal?" Pawel asked when the waitress had gone.

Kamal tensed and remained silent. What was he doing in this smelly, smokey room filled with strangers? What was he doing sitting with this guy who asked too many questions? Back in Iraq, the wrong people, Saddam Hussein's people, were always asking questions.

"You leave Country Gardens awful sudden," Pawel said. "One day, you there no more. Last day I seeing you was day you cut your hand."

"I get new job."

"Ahhh. At shopping plaza."

Two glass mugs arrived at the table. Golden meant beer, Kamal realized, looking at the glass of liquid in front of him. The colour was beautiful, a golden amber. He suddenly felt thirsty. He wanted to pick up the mug and pour the liquid down his throat. Don't be stupid, he told himself. The Quran forbade alcohol. If he picked up this mug it would be the first step into sin. The Crazy Lady's voice filled the room again. What was she singing? Something about feeling lonely and feeling blue.

Pawel poured half the liquid in his mug down his throat and wiped his mouth with the back of his hand.

"You liking your new job, Kamal? You big boss at shopping plaza? I bet you making lots of money."

"Is part-time job only." Kamal's friend, Saad, had found him the job at the plaza when the garden centre laid off its summer help. But he was still living in the shadows.

"Where you living, Kamal?"

Kamal wasn't going to tell Pawel that the apartment he shared with Saad was less than a mile away. "Other side of Toronto," he said. "Near the airport."

"Mario telling me you see Dr. Edno when you cut your hand."

"So? I cut hand pruning roses. I get stitches."

"Dr. Edno, he fixing up workers with no papers. He taking cash and keeping his mouth quiet."

"Maybe. I not know." Kamal could feel Pawel's pale green eyes boring into him. He kept his own eyes on the mug on the table.

"Country Gardens take workers with no papers. Paying them cash."

"Yeah?" Kamal licked his dry lips. The beer looked inviting. He could almost feel the golden liquid sliding down his throat, filling him with the sunshine this frozen country lacked.

"If government finding out, going be big trouble. Country Gardens owners pay big fine. Workers in even bigger trouble. Having to go back to their country. Me, I not having that problem. I got contacts. Good contacts. Immigration not bothering me."

Kamal reached out and wrapped his right hand around the mug. The glass was cold but he could still feel the golden sunshine seeping into his hand. A sunshine that burned like ice.

Pawel drained his mug and laughed. "Drink up, Kamal. What the matter with you? I already finishing." He waved at the waitress.

"Where you from, Kamal? I forgetting."

"Iraq." Kamal remembered Pawel telling him he was from Poland.

"Iraq. Saddam Hussein, that maniac, running Iraq. I thinking you not want go back there. Americans going bomb hell outta Iraq."

The summer before, Kamal was visiting Saad in Toronto when Saddam invaded Kuwait. "You can't get on that plane," Saad told him the day before his return flight. "You spoke out against Saddam. Now he's making his big push, he'll crush dissenters like ants under his feet."

Kamal never showed up for his flight. Now it was January and the United States was demanding Saddam pull out of Kuwait. Pawel was right. He couldn't go back.

He took the mug by the handle and raised it to his lips. His nostrils twitched. The beer had a strong, yeasty smell. He parted his lips and poured liquid into his mouth. It tasted bitter. He gulped down several mouthfuls and set the mug back on the table. His stomach churned. He sat up straight, willing his guts to hold still. He felt warmth rising from his belly and sweat breaking out on his neck and face. He had tasted the forbidden.

The Crazy Lady, Patsy Somebody, started singing again. Her voice wrapped itself around his mind.

The waitress arrived with two more mugs. Pawel held one up, as if to make a toast.

Kamal picked up his mug again. But his hand was shaking so much that beer spilled over the table.

"Hey, what you doing, wasting good beer?" Pawel cried.

Kamal pulled his wallet from his jacket pocket. "How much this Golden?"

"My treat, Kamal. I buying you drink."

Kamal placed a five-dollar bill on the table. "Gotta go."

"Kamal, listen—"

"Getting late." Kamal darted to the door and tripped on the mat at the entrance.

Outside, he broke into a run. He ran two blocks, then turned in behind a convenience store and rested his forehead against the cold brick wall. He cursed himself. He had done the forbidden. He had lost control and succumbed to temptation. He had polluted his body and his soul.

And he had Pawel to worry about.

"Kamal, we meeting again! Two times in one week."

For three days, Kamal had been looking for another job. A job where Pawel wouldn't be able to find him. He'd scanned the ads in The Toronto Star, but he knew these jobs were not for illegals. Saad told him he'd ask around, but so far he hadn't come up with anything.

He wanted to ignore Pawel. Finish up his work and head back to the apartment.

"A drink tonight, Kamal? I having time for one drink with you. You almost finish here, I think."

What if he refused? The fear of being deported sent Kamal's mind racing. Pawel suspected he was working illegally. He could go to the authorities and tell them where to find him. Kamal would find himself on the next plane to Iraq.

"I go change my clothes," he said to Pawel. "I come back in five minutes."

The bar was crowded. The tables were filled with men and women unwinding after a week of work.

"Friday night, lots of people here," Pawel said as they squeezed themselves into chairs at an empty table near the back door.

Friday, Kamal thought bitterly. He should have been at the mosque but he'd completely forgotten. He'd fallen that low.

"Hi, guys," the red-skirted waitress sang out. "What'll it be tonight?"

"Molson Canadian." Pawel winked at Kamal. "Canadian like you, eh, Kamal?"

"Golden," Kamal said. "I take Golden."

"So, Kamal, you got yourself sorted out?" Pawel asked when the beer arrived at the table.

The back of Kamal's neck tingled. "What you mean?"

"You having no papers when you work at Country Gardens."

"Why you say that?"

"Worker going to Dr. Edno has no papers. Everybody knowing that. You having no papers then and I thinking you having no papers now."

Kamal took a sip of his Golden, then downed half the liquid in the glass.

"You knowing what they do to people they catch working with no papers? They sending them back where they from. I thinking you not want to be going back to Iraq. But listen, Kamal. Jola got cousin who helping friends. You understand?"

Kamal felt warmth rising from his stomach. Suddenly, he felt very warm all over and he considered removing his jacket. No, he'd go as soon as he got Pawel to leave him alone. He tried to think of something to convince him he wasn't an illegal, but with the laughter and music around him, and the beer sending heat waves through his body, his brain wasn't working properly.

"You think 'bout what I saying, Kamal."

What was he talking about?

51

"Bit expensive. But worth it. You no more need be hiding." Pawel glanced at his wrist watch. "How 'bout I meeting you here Monday, Kamal? I bringing Jola's cousin. He making you deal you can't refuse."

Kamal's brain cleared. So that was it; Pawel wanted money. He wanted Kamal to pay him to keep quiet. But if he gave Pawel money, he'd be admitting he was an illegal. He'd never be free of him.

Pawel rose, clapped him on the shoulder and threw a ten-dollar bill and a loonie on the table.

"My treat, Kamal. I seeing you here Monday night. What time you finishing work? Nine? I meeting you here nine o'clock."

Fear clutched Kamal's belly. Who was this cousin of Jola's? Was he from Immigration? Was he paying Pawel to turn him in?

Pawel went out the back door and Kamal dashed after him.

Outside, he found himself in a narrow alley behind the building. Kamal reached into his jacket pocket and took out his Swiss army knife. He opened the knife and held it behind his back. "Pawel!" he called. "Wait."

Pawel turned. "What the matter, Kamal? You not looking so hot. Go home, yes?"

"What deal you talk about?"

"I forgetting. Have something for you," Pawel said, taking his wallet out of his jacket pocket and searching through it. "Jola write list for you. You bringing this Monday night."

Kamal stepped behind him. He held his breath and summoned up all his strength. With his left arm, he reached under Pawel's chin and pulled his head backwards. With his right hand, he plunged the knife deep into the side of Pawel's neck. Pawel lurched forward, making a gasping sound. Kamal raised his hands over his head into a fist and brought it down as hard as he could on the back of Pawel's head. Pawel crumpled on the pavement in front of him.

Kamal glanced around. The alley was deserted. He pulled the knife from Pawel's neck and wiped it with a tissue. His jacket was covered with blood. He touched his face; it felt sticky.

A window in the bar opened and Kamal stepped into the shadows. He waited a couple of minutes, but nobody came out. Inside, the Crazy Lady started singing.

He needed time. How long would it be before the police arrived? How long before they started asking if Pawel had been seen with anyone?

But what if they didn't know it was Pawel? His wallet! If his wallet was missing, it could be a long time before the police identified the body.

He found the wallet on the pavement beside Pawel and picked it up.

He crept along the side of the building and ran across the street. If he kept to the back streets and parking lots, away from traffic, he'd get to the apartment in about ten minutes. He'd throw his jacket into the dumpster and wash up in the basement. Tomorrow, he would leave Toronto. He'd head for somewhere far away. Calgary, maybe.

He paused to catch his breath, leaning against a cold brick back wall. He remembered the wallet in his hand and opened it.

There wasn't much cash. Thirty dollars, maybe. A folded paper slipped from between the bills and fell to the ground. Kamal scooped it up and opened it.

Passport photo
Place of birth
Date of birth

Colour of eyes

A photo

So Jola's cousin could make papers for Kamal.

A tear ran down his cheek and he squeezed his eyes shut. He slumped against the wall and dropped the paper.

He wept while the Crazy Lady sang in his head.

Poky's Christmas Cookies
Ken Loomes

It was impossible to walk quietly. The snow was squeaking and crunching so loudly that Poky was certain every dog on the reserve would start barking. He didn't want the noise to wake up his little sister. He wanted to surprise her with the cookies.

As he walked, he looked back over his shoulder. He wasn't really afraid of wild animals but ever since his mother had told him to stop looking at everything and stop being so poky or the wolves would get him, he often checked behind him.

Snow was getting in his runners when his feet sunk into the drifts that were sometimes up to his knees. He was glad that it had snowed even though it was hard to walk. Miss Ralston wouldn't be able to get out until the road was plowed and that meant she had time to help him make cookies.

He walked past the school, closed now for the holidays. It was still and silent except for smoke coming from the chimney. Poky didn't think he had ever heard this much quiet before. Smoke was coming out of the chimneys at Sinclair's and Anderson's and other places. It seemed the whole world was snow and silence and smoke coming from chimneys.

He wanted to stop and watch the pale streamers drifting above the roofs of houses. It was going almost straight up, but sometimes curling in the still morning air and then going straight again until it disappeared into the sky. Poky wished he had remembered to bring some coloured pencils home from school. He would like to draw a picture of the houses and the grey-white smoke against the green trees and blue sky. The man from the city who had come to inspect the school said he was very good. Get some coloured pencils, the man had said; they're better than crayons. His teacher had shown him a picture of a big box of pencils. She said there was almost fifty. Poky had hoped he might get them for Christmas, but he knew now that he wouldn't. Maybe next year he would ask again.

He tried to walk in the footprints his uncle had made when he came to their place late yesterday. Sometimes he had to take two steps, then just a short step and a little jump, so he found it was easier to make his own trail.

Poky wished he had mittens. He put one hand in his pocket and held on to the small bag of flour and the bowl of sugar with his other. After a few steps he changed hands, wondering if he should stop and open his jacket and somehow balance the open bowl inside so he could put both hands in his pockets. It wasn't much farther to the nursing station. If she answered the door right away it would be okay. Poky wasn't sure if she would let him in. There was nothing wrong with him or anyone in his family. He had no reason to go there, yet she told him if he ever needed anything to come and see her. He would stand back after he knocked on her door so she could see him and wouldn't be afraid.

He almost turned around and ran home after he knocked the second time and heard no sounds from inside. She couldn't have gone away; there were no tracks in the fresh snow. There was lots of smoke coming out of the chimney. Maybe she would laugh at him anyway. All he wanted to do was find out how to make cookies like the ones she had made for their Christmas concert. They were the best that Poky had ever eaten, so soft they would melt in your mouth like snow, so warm and sweet he wanted to eat them all. His little sister had cried because she wanted more too, but they were all gone. He asked Miss Ralston how she made them and she just laughed and said, "Oh, you need some flour and sugar and some other things and you mix it all together, and put it in the oven, and out come cookies." Well, he had the flour and the sugar. All he needed was to know how to mix it together.

There had been no cereal left in the box when he got up. Poky could see that his mom had cooked all the eggs for his uncle and his father sometime last night and the bread was all gone too. He was so hungry all he could think about was the goodies and the new pencils that must be in the suitcase on the floor beside his sleeping uncle. His Mom and Dad had been talking about something that his uncle was going to bring, but when he tried to get closer to listen they stopped talking. He knew then that it must be something for Christmas for him and his sister.

Poky knew he shouldn't look in something that belonged to someone else but he would just have one tiny piece of candy or whatever was in there and leave the rest until everyone was up. Quietly, so he wouldn't wake anyone, he crept along the floor to the suitcase. It was right beside the couch where his uncle was sleeping, his arm hanging down just inches away from the top of the big brown case.

Poky stopped and stared at the big snake tattoo on his uncle's arm. It was red and green and had its mouth open. He could see the two long sharp fangs that were dripping blood. His uncle shifted his arm and it looked like the snake was moving. Poky sat back, his heart racing. Slowly, he opened the suitcase. There wasn't any candy or presents or food, just shirts and pants. All he could see besides clothes was a small bag of flour. It wasn't in a paper bag like they got at the store. It was in the same kind of plastic bag as some worker's kept their sandwiches.

Just flour. He couldn't eat just flour. Then he thought: he brought it to make cookies. Did his uncle know how to make cookies? His mom had made cookies once, but they were so hard that no one could eat them. The only person that he knew could make cookies was Miss Ralston at the nursing station.

He knocked once more on the door and was about to go home when he heard something inside.

"Who's there?"

"It's Alvin." He could see Miss Ralston's eye as she looked through the narrow crack.

"What's the matter?" She asked.

"Nothing." Poky said. "Nobody's bleeding or nothing."

"What are you here for, then?"

Poky looked down at his feet. It was stupid to come. He wanted to throw the flour and sugar in a snow bank and go home. If his hands weren't so cold he would have turned and run away. He wanted to put his hand out to get it warm in the heat he could feel sneaking out the tiny gap in the door. He pulled his hand out of his jacket so he could put the other one in, carefully so she wouldn't see the bag.

"What's that?" She asked.

"Flour." He said, still looking down at his shoes.

"I didn't hear you."

Poky said it again. He thought she still didn't hear him, as she didn't say anything for a long time. "Why did you bring flour?"

"So you could show me how to make cookies."

He heard her kicking at the old towels around the bottom of the door and telling him to come in.

"I brought sugar too," he said, as he handed her the bowl. "I want to make cookies for my sister for Christmas." His head was down and he was speaking so softly that Miss Ralston had to ask him twice what he had said.

"Cookies?" She finally said.

"Like you made." His head coming up to look at her for the first time. "You said you put flour and sugar in the oven and got out cookies. I was going to make them, but I didn't know how."

"I see," Miss Ralston said slowly.

"Come, stand by the stove. I'll make you some hot chocolate."

Dishes and spoons rattled in the kitchen as Miss Ralston put things on the counter. Poky stood in front of the nice, warm fire sipping slowly at the hot chocolate that had lots of milk in it. He wanted to go and see what she was doing so he could do it when he was bigger, but she had told him to stay by the stove. The noise of her sitting down heavily in a chair made him look around. She was sitting holding the bag in her hands, staring at it, her face almost white as the snow.

"Where did you get this, … flour?"

He was hoping she wouldn't ask that. He put his head down again not wanting to say he took it out of the suitcase. He moved his feet, feeling warm all of a sudden. He looked out of the corner of his eyes and could see she was holding on to the bag tightly or he would have grabbed it and run home.

"It's okay, you can tell me."

"My uncle," Poky said as loudly as he could, so he wouldn't have to say it again.

"I see," she said.

"Did your uncle give you this flour?"

Poky put his head down again. Why did she have to ask all these questions? "No," he said in a tiny little voice. Miss Ralston was standing close behind him, listening for his answer. Slowly, he told her that he was looking for something to eat and had found the flour in the suitcase.

"Does he know you have it?"

"No, everybody's still sleeping."

She was quiet for a long time. Then she said, "This isn't the right kind of flour."

The only sound in the small house was when a log snapped in the fire. Poky knew she was still standing beside him, but she wasn't moving or even asking any more questions. He wanted to turn and look at her, but he kept his hands out in front of him and his eyes on the top of the stove.

"I'll make some cookies, but I'll have to use my own flour. Give me a couple of minutes and you can take this bag and put it where you found it and then come back here and help me make the cookies. You just stay at the stove for now and keep warm, okay."

Poky didn't know why he had to make an extra trip, but if she was making cookies it would be worth it. He turned just a little so he could see her out of the corner of his eye. He saw her take some small boxes out of one cupboard and some bowls out of another. He looked a minute later and could see some flour in a bowl and Miss Ralston dumping a box of white powder into the plastic bag. He had no idea why she was filling the bag with flour when it already had flour in it. She was always looking over to see if he was watching her, but she would turn her shoulders just a bit before she looked so he knew when to face back to the stove.

"There, you can take this back now. Put it back where you found it and then come back here." She grabbed his arm and added, "Do you think anybody will be awake?"

"No, not for a long time yet."

"Okay, see you in a bit. Wait. Here put this jacket on and these mittens. You can bring them back when you come." She smiled at him then.

Poky was glad to see that. She had looked so worried before, like she didn't really want to help.

He was back in no time. Miss Ralston had put on jeans and a heavy sweater while he was gone.

"We're all ready. You can wash your hands really well, okay. Go in the bathroom. There's soap and hot water, then you can help me."

She must have been in here recently because there was a fine dust of flour around the toilet bowl. She must have spilled some on the floor too.

Cookies had a lot more than flour and sugar. Miss Ralston mixed up all the ingredients and he helped her put them on cookie sheets. Then she cut up some red and green cherries to put on top and baked them in the oven. It was fun to make them, and the best part was that he got to take them home.

Poky wanted to do something besides just saying thank you. When he got back to school he would draw her a picture of the houses with smoke coming out the chimneys. He would put the nursing station in the centre and a small boy with a plate of cookies walking through the snow. He didn't want her to ever forget the day she helped him make Christmas cookies.

Circumcision Through Words

Mark Foss

Friends of Africa is cutting back so much it won't pay for a hotel room the night before the conference. Murray has to take the Ottawa-Montreal bus early in the morning. As he quietly gets dressed, he watches Lisa's face twitch and her mouth voice words he can't quite make out.

Last night she was in tears again about her sister. Margo hasn't been answering her telephone or responding to Lisa's messages. Their mother hasn't heard from her in a week, and the restaurant manager said Margo had quit her job.

"I'm worried," Lisa had said. "She might have gone off the deep end. Will you try to reach her tomorrow? Maybe go by her place after the conference?"

"Sure. I can do that."

"Thanks Murray." Her voice broke a little, and once again he was surprised at the emotion. In the same room together, Lisa and Margo can't show each other any love. Apart, though, Lisa frets about her all the time. Sometimes, when Lisa talks in her sleep, Murray picks up the thread of her nightmares. She sees Margo driving home drunk and slamming into a hydro pole, killing herself just the way their father did. He doesn't wake her, because he thinks

63

she needs to work it through, but he does put his arm around her until her breathing slips back to normal. This is the best part of their relationship—the comforting.

He dozes on the bus, waking only when it pulls into the station. A quick ride on the Metro and he reaches the university, finding the conference room without any trouble. He registers, picking up a binder and a "Hello, my name is..." sticker. At a quiet seat in the back, he takes off his winter coat. He writes his name and sticks the tag to the lapel of his jacket. Then he watches the other participants file in. This being a conference on female genital mutilation, they are mostly black women. Short, fat, tall, plain, attractive, they arrive in groups of twos and threes. He assumes they're all Africans, or African-Canadians. Have they bonded so quickly or did they already know each other? A few black men arrive, followed by a handful of white women. Murray seems to be the only white man in the room. He suddenly feels conspicuous sitting by himself so he opens his binder and reviews the agenda. After the morning plenary and lunch, he's signed up for the Health Effects workshop.

The chairperson, a matronly African with grizzled hair, taps the microphone. In both official languages, she urges people to find a place so they can begin. A few seats down from Murray, a young black woman with cornrow braids sits by herself. She slips her knapsack onto the empty chair beside her, as if she's saving it for someone, but no one joins her.

In the plenary, three panellists raise the various issues to be discussed in working groups. It's the usual suspects: health effects, FGM and AIDS, education campaigns. What's different, to his mind, is the inclusion of Doctor Ogunsola, an African physician originally from Nigeria who now practises in Montreal. He's heavy-set, and talks with a good deal of swagger. Many women whisper in their seats, shaking their heads at this display. Even the chairperson looks uncomfortable sitting at the same table with him.

"Women have to start taking responsibility for this horrific practice," says Doctor Ogunsola. "The African men won't talk about it, as you know too well. It is up to you. Mothers are to blame. They must be educated."

"Who are you to blame the mothers?" a woman in the audience shouts back at him. A few other women cry out in agreement.

"Who would you blame then? The fathers?" the doctor retorts. His eyes search the crowd to find the heckler.

"The doctors," someone else shouts.

"I don't think we need to blame anyone," the chairperson says. "Please let the doctor finish his remarks. There will be plenty of time for discussion in the workshops."

"Thank you, Madame Chair," the doctor says. He gloats a little, pulling the microphone closer to his mouth.

"In my practice, I have seen too many young girls living in Canada who have been forced to undertake this barbaric exercise. There is no excuse for it in this country. None whatsoever."

"What do you know about it?" a voice calls out. It's the young woman with the braids. She stands up. "Let me tell you something. All of my African friends in Toronto had it done. My mother thought she was protecting me, but she made me an outcast.

My friends rejected me. If I had the choice, I would have it done today."

As she sits down, the room is filled with an angry buzz, but this time it's not directed at the doctor. "You are a stupid girl," someone calls out. Heads turn toward the young woman who sits there defiantly, returning all the hard gazes. The African doctor shakes his head at the woman, in a sad, patronizing way. "You do not understand what you're saying," he says into the microphone.

"Please. Everyone," says the chairperson. "This is a very sensitive issue. We know that. That's why we're here. To work together to find solutions."

After a few minutes, the plenary continues. One panellist, a white woman from a UN agency, talks about FGM as a human rights issue. Another panellist, an African woman from Kenya, talks about an alternative to FGM called "circumcision through words." It's an approach that Friends of Africa has already started to support—a week-long rite of passage for young women that finishes with a "coming of age day" where the entire community joins in for music, dance and feasting.

It's all interesting, but by this time, most people aren't able to sit still. A few people still steal glances at the woman with the cornbraids, sneering at her or else shaking their heads with pity. When the woman happens to look his way, Murray sees the name on her tag is Kiddisti. He tries to be affirming with a small, tight-lipped smile. She smiles back.

"These women, they make me sick," Kiddisti says, stabbing a piece of cauliflower with her fork. "No one ever says anything out loud, but it's like they have a club. If you're not mutilated, you can't join. You don't even have the right to talk to them.

This is what makes me so angry. I have felt this way all my life, always pushed to the outside."

Kiddisti and Murray sit together with their buffet lunch in a far corner of the cafeteria, away from the other participants who clump together in the centre of the room. Her body, which Murray had thought was simply slender, is flat and angular, almost anorexic. Her long face and her mouth, with its crooked bottom teeth and thin lips, make her appear tough, but he can see sadness in her dark eyes. Sadness and vulnerability. His heart flutters a little, sitting alone with her. If someone came to join them, he would tell them to go somewhere else. Only outsiders belong here.

"I have never felt at home in Canada," she says. "So I finally went back to Eritrea two years ago, to see if I could live there. I hadn't been home since I left in the 1970s."

"You left when the war started with Ethiopia?"

"That's right," she says, sharply. Her eyes challenge his face for signs of judgment. "I had an uncle in Toronto, and he took us in—my mother, brother and me. But I still had lots of family in Asmara. I went to see them. They were polite, but it was obvious I didn't fit in. My accent, my clothes. Behind their smiles, they were angry. My aunts had all lost sons during the war. They never forgave my mother for leaving. I think they resented me for being alive. It was clear to me I could never go back."

"That's very sad," he says.

"I'm over it now," she says quickly. "I'm happy here at McGill doing African Studies." He's not convinced, but he doesn't challenge her.

"So why did your organization send you to this conference?"

"To learn more about FGM. It's the theme for our fundraising campaign next fall." As he says the words, he hears how shallow they sound.

"The theme," she repeats, raising an eyebrow.

"I'll be writing most of the materials," he says. "Otherwise they would have sent one of the program staff."

"So they sent the white guy to learn about FGM," she says in a teasing voice.

"That's right. I feel a little out of place here, I can tell you."

"Good," she says. "You should."

Silence for a moment, as they finish up their lunch.

"Do you have any Africans working with you?"

"We used to. She went back to Nigeria."

"Huh," she says, with a sneer. "Good for her."

There's another awkward silence so he reaches into his pocket for a business card.

"If you ever come to Ottawa, stop by the office," he says.

Their fingers touch as they exchange the card, and it sends a shiver of possibility down his spine.

"Thanks," she says. "I will."

"We should go now. It's getting on. Which workshop are you in?"

"Education Strategies."

"Me too," he says, lying.

She smiles warmly.

"Good," she says. "It will be nice to have a friend in the room."

As they enter the room for the workshop, his heart sinks a little. Doctor Ogunsola is there. Kiddisti chooses a chair directly opposite the doctor, as if to show she's not afraid of him. He looks up from his binder for a second, then lowers his gaze again. The

other six or seven participants are all African women, and they look curiously at Murray as he sits beside Kiddisti. The fiercest glance is from the young
woman two seats down from Kiddisti. With her
light skin, he wonders if the woman is Ethiopian,
and if this will create another conflict with Kiddisti.
He's glad there's an empty chair between them.

A middle-aged African woman standing at the
front writes "Education Strategies" in block letters
on a flipchart, then turns to face everyone at the
table.

"Welcome everyone," she says. "My name is
Dorothy, and I'm the facilitator. Can we have a go-
around to introduce ourselves? Just your name and
your organization. I'd also like a volunteer to take
notes as we go along." She sits down and picks up a
pen. As the names are called out, she ticks them off a
list. The light-skinned woman, whose name is Gelila,
offers to take notes.

Dorothy scans her list after Murray says his name
aloud.

"Murray Lockhart," she repeats. "I don't seem to
have you here. Is this where you're supposed to be?"

He can feel everyone focused on him. Even Kiddisti has turned her head slightly, waiting for his answer.

"This is where I want to be."

"All right then," Dorothy says, coldly.

After the go-around, Dorothy recaps the presenta-
tion from the Kenyan woman on "circumcision
through words." She asks them to consider how to
transfer the spirit of this approach to those African
communities in Canada that still believe in FGM. At
first, the talk is polite, but eventually it gets heated
again.

"I think we need to go straight to the girls themselves," says Gelila. "We need to empower them to make their own decisions, to show them they have choices."

Doctor Ogunsola shakes his head dismissively.

"No, no, no," he says. "It's very well to say that, but the fact of the matter is, these girls are like sheep. They will do what their mothers and their grandmothers tell them. You have to reach the mothers first. In my practice..."

"We know all about your practice," says Kiddisti, interrupting. "You obviously treat women like animals."

"Please," Dorothy says. "Can we stay on the topic?"

"Your mother was right to protect you," Doctor Ogunsola says, looking squarely at Kiddisti. "But I don't know if you deserved it."

Several of the women draw in their breath sharply, and Gelila slams her pen down on the table. "Who are you to say that to her?" she says. "You call yourself a doctor?"

Dr. Ogunsola's mouth opens, but then he stops himself.

"You're right," he says, finally. "It was very unprofessional of me, and very unkind. I apologize," he says, looking at Kiddisti. "It's just that I feel very strongly about this. My wife took our daughter to her village in Nigeria. My mother-in-law, she went behind our backs. They used a razor blade, and Ajayi died. She bled to death." His voice chokes at the words, and he lowers his face toward the table.

A hushed, uncomfortable silence fills the room.

"I am sorry for you," Kiddisti says, finally, holding back tears. Dr. Ogunsola nods his head without looking up.

"Why don't we take a break for a few minutes?" Dorothy says. Before Murray can get up, Gelila has offered Kiddisti a tissue to dry her eyes.

"It's horrible, isn't it?" Gelila says. "How this affects everyone in different ways."

Kiddisti nods, dabbing her eyes.

"I'm going to the washroom," Gelila says. "Do you want to come?"

Kiddisti nods and follows her out of the room. The other women file out as well, leaving Doctor Ogunsola and Murray alone in the room. The doctor keeps his head down, dabbing his eyes with a handkerchief.

"Is there anything I can do?" Murray says, quietly.

"Can you bring her back?" he snaps. His glare makes Murray flush.

As the doctor leaves, Murray keeps his eyes cast downward. The empty room just reinforces the hollow feeling inside his gut so he gets up, and walks aimlessly in the hall for a few minutes. Then he remembers Margo. She's not there so he leaves a message on her answering machine that says he'll try again later, before he heads home. Once he returns to the meeting room, he sees that Gelila has filled the empty chair next to Kiddisti, and the two of them are talking quietly together. They seem to have become fast friends. The other women arrive, but the doctor's chair remains empty.

"Doctor Ogunsola decided to leave," Dorothy tells them. "He said it was too much for him to come back. He didn't feel it was right for him to stay."

Several of the women cluck in protest while others nod their heads sadly. Kiddisti and Gelila start talking even more intensely. Murray wonders if his offer to help pushed the doctor over the edge. He wishes now that he'd left too. For the next hour, the women talk about ways to reach elders, mothers and children. They talk about reaching African doctors, community development workers and politicians. Murray offers a few words of advice about influencing news media, but for the most part, he just listens. By the end, Gelila has filled five sheets of flipchart paper with ideas and strategies. As the workshop draws to a close, Dorothy asks for a volunteer to present their report to plenary.

"I nominate Kiddisti," Gelila says. A few of the other women nod in approval.

"Oh, I don't know," Kiddisti begins.

"I can help you make sense of my writing," Gelila says.

"Yes, you do it," one of the women says.

"All right," Kiddisti says, smiling shyly.

"That's settled then," Dorothy says. "Good work everyone. See you in plenary in fifteen minutes." With those words, the women start talking among themselves again. Kiddisti and Gelila remove the flipchart paper that's taped to the walls. Murray folds up his binder, gathers his coat and leaves the room quickly, unnoticed.

At the pay telephone in the hall, he tries Margo again. This time she's home.

"Murray," she says. "I was hoping you'd call back soon."

"Lisa's been worried."

"She is such a mother hen," Margo says, laughing. "I've been away with an old boyfriend in Florida."

"But you quit your job."

"I got a better one, closer to home. I start on Friday."

"Oh. That's good."

"I think so."

"Well, I'll tell Lisa the good news when I get home. Do you have time for a coffee?"

"Actually, Brad and I just got back. We're pretty wiped out."

"That's all right. Another time."

He hangs up the telephone, feeling a little let down. Other participants head back into the main room for the final plenary. He doesn't see Gelila or Kiddisti, but he's sure they're together. They're probably already making plans for dinner tonight. He decides to cut out early and head home. As he buttons up his coat, he sees the name tag still stuck on the lapel of his suit. The upside down letters look strange, and he silently mouths his name the way it should sound, as if to reassure himself that the two words are not part of some foreign language beyond his grasp.

Abe
Sheila Howe

I pressed the awkward yellow plastic down until it bit into my skull and checked one last time for my gloves and goggles. They were still there, tucked securely in my lap. The car slowed to a stop as I grabbed my bucket and bag and climbed out the door. "Thanks for the ride." I looked at my watch. "I'll wait for you here. Five o'clock."

As my lifeline pulled away, I waved my hand slowly like the flag on a sinking ship. How I wished instead that I could be pulled back, to him, to what I knew. The churning in my stomach sent waves of nausea through my body. But there was no time for pity. I had to be ready.

Wilfully, as if in slow motion, I turned to survey the scene. It looked all too familiar. Debris littered the site. A league of men, armed with hammers, crowbars and shovels surrounded the shell of a building. Gusts of brown dirt cast a dull, dusty sheen on the landscape as particles of insulation and sawdust swirled in the dry heat of a relentless wind. And yet, somehow, the chaos made me feel right at home. The hot sun welcomed me too, with a comforting warmth on the bit of exposed dark skin above the collar of my stiff, new uniform. I was surprised at its intensity on the tail end of September.

"Are you the new guy?" The solid looking man at the top of the scaffold brought my attention back to the moment. "I'll be right there." He clambered down skillfully and sprang off the bottom rung. He sprinted towards me with a powerful stride and an easy confidence I envied. I wondered what I had gotten myself into.

"Hello." I offered him my hand and he shook it heartily. He looked at my hat. "Abe!"

I managed a confused smile. "Pardon?" He pointed to the label hastily applied to the peak.

"Johnny sent you." A backhoe roared by and I jumped quickly to the side.

"Mr. Johnny. Yes. He told me to come at eight." I looked nervously at the bustling scene. "Am I late?" I shouted over the noise.

"Today is orientation." He gestured to follow him. As we made our way down the ruts of the muddy path, he turned to me. His smile was reassuring. "My name is Nick. I'll show you the ropes." The demolition continued as we rounded the corner of the building. He pointed to a mound of rubble, and winked. "I always save a special job for the first day!"

The morning passed quickly enough. I had arranged several piles of lumber into neat stacks. The afternoon would be spent organizing the bricks and lathing, by myself, again. I wiped the sweat from my forehead as the rest of the crew sauntered by.

"Going for pizza?"

I returned a blank stare. The young man wearing a bandanna and fatigues looked at me as if I were a fool. "Leave him alone," he told his friend. "He's weird!"

It would take time to understand their ways. But the hunger pangs in my belly reminded me that I must concentrate first on finding a place to eat. I picked up my bucket and looked around. I quickly gathered some discarded ceiling tiles and set them against the remnants of a door. I added pieces of particleboard and assembled odd bits of lumber. A flimsy piece of fibreglass rested on top, anchored with a two by four. Time for lunch—I was famished.

As I was about to pour my tea, I spotted Nick crawling through the makeshift tunnel towards me. "This is quite the set up!" he said on entering the eating area. "Wonderful!" He tried to straighten up in the tight quarters. "I get it—the long entrance keeps out the wind." He looked around with admiration. "It's downright brilliant! What do you call it?" I fumbled for an answer.

"There is no name. It is okay that I used these things?" But he went on about the ingenuity of design, out of scraps! I took my cave for granted. It was more practical than remarkable. "It is custom to have protection from the sun and the dust. Food stays clean and the meal is pleasant. And it is for social time. Will you join me?"

Nick looked at the cement block lying nearby. He studied my posture for a minute and then slowly lowered himself onto it, trying his best to imitate my traditional squat. The water in the pot hissed as I turned the cylinder on the propane stove. He watched in awe as I pulled a delicate porcelain cup and saucer from my bucket and filled it.

"What next?" he laughed. "Are you going to pull a rabbit out of your hard hat?" I glared at the label and scowled. He didn't miss a trick. "Hat doesn't fit?" I looked at him, unsure how much I should reveal.

"No," I replied. "My name is Abdul."

He raised his hand as I attempted to pass him the cup. "First things first!" He reached into the bulging pocket of his jacket. He fished through the tape measures and tools and pulled out a marker. He tore off the label and began to write. "That's better!" he said with a satisfied smile. "Now, how about that tea!" And as he savoured the spicy, sweet drink, I studied Nick's work. "ABDUL" was now proudly engraved on the front.

At the end of the day, I slipped into the cave and changed into clean wool pants and replaced my dirty work boots with a pair of shiny black oxfords. When I emerged, Nick was waiting. I looked at him anxiously.

"Are you expecting to be paid tonight?" I nodded, ashamed at my impatience. He reached into his pants and placed some money in my hand. I counted out forty-seven dollars, my wages for eight-and-a-half hard hours. "That's seven dollars an hour, right?"

But I didn't understand. I was expecting more. "How many taxes you have in Canada?" I asked. He clenched his jaw and sighed.

"Didn't Johnny explain?"

I looked up sheepishly. "Every penny is important."

Gently, he extracted the contents of my fist. He pulled out his wallet and added three blue bills. "Take this. I'll deal with Johnny later." His exasperation slowly melted into a grin.

"You did a fine job today. Could you come back tomorrow?" I nodded eagerly. "How would you like to work for me? Hell, the tea and tent alone are worth eighty bucks a day!" I grasped his hand with gratitude. And as I turned to leave, I'm not sure who noticed the tear in each man's eye.

How blessed am I! Though it is not my engineering work, this job promises to be better than I expected. My body has surprised me with its hidden strength and endurance. Money pads my pocket and I have made a good friend. Soon my generous brother-in-law will return, kind enough to share his car and his home. I look presentable and I am proud to return there to share the story of this first day with my family.

Life here will be a challenge, but now I do not mind so much to be far away from the other chaos, with its searing wind and indelible dirt and an interminable fear, where I lived only fifteen days ago; in Afghanistan, the country that I, Abdul, my beautiful wife and my five brave children called home on September 11, 2001.

The Mangohattan
James Romanow

"Something to drink sir?" The waiter put a basket of corn chips on the table with an earthenware bowl of chili dip.

"A Tanqueray and Schweppes. With a squeeze of lime please." Indians have been forging bad copies of the "By appointment to Her Majesty" seal for a hundred years. You'll find them stuck on everything from jam to gin. If you aren't specific, you are likely to be served alcohol from a green bottle labelled Dankeray. Inevitably the tonic will be called Schwebs.

A band began to shuffle equipment on the stage. One of them had the striking beauty that you sometimes see, a beauty that transcends sex. I imagined that he was the lead singer, and that most of his talent went into his well-defined physique. The band wore team shorts, suspenders and American trainers. They did not wear shirts. Given the heat and humidity of Bombay in early October, it was a sensible costume. I had done my best to sit as far from the bandstand as possible, but modern amplification would make it unlikely Janet and I would enjoy much conversation while they played.

The crowd were children of the upper class, what you would expect to find in a Mexican restaurant in

Bombay: pure Bollywood manqué. Although the patio was lit only by torches on bamboo stakes, a good half of the crowd wore shades, also with designer labels. The average age was maybe twenty-five, with a sprinkling of older men on the prowl. The dress code was western designer jeans with men's white dress shirts. Depending on the wearer's sex, the shirts were either unbuttoned down to the sternum or untucked, with the tails tied in a knot to the same point. In either case, there was enough sleek skin and toned muscle on display to make me feel old, flabby and out of place.

Mind you, I have never been truly comfortable in these kinds of establishments, even when I was the right age. I was always the kid on the edge of the dance floor, watching the children of the ruling class in their graceful minuet.

Janet did not suffer from those fears. She was able to accept gifts of adoration with a flash of a smile. To be fair to her, this kind of place had not been Janet's scene as we said then. I was surprised she had chosen it as the setting for a pair of forty-somethings to get reacquainted.

I hadn't seen her in more than two decades. Back then, she would easily have eclipsed even this crowd. I wondered if she had maintained her figure. She had a streak of vanity. However, she had never had to work at how she looked. I found it hard to imagine her pounding away in a health club, with the determination of a salmon swimming upstream.

For Janet was beautiful, the most beautiful woman I had ever known. Before she became religious, she had wanted to be a dancer. She had not been one of the willowy anorexics so beloved by directors, and this had probably been her undoing as a dancer. It struck me that this was the perfect place for her to reappear. The pronounced curves of her figure, and her abundant black hair were quite normal here.

I never knew why she picked me. She was the object of desire for every boy in the school. Not only was I in no way remarkable, I hadn't been capable of carrying off the relationship. My fear of getting caught by her parents rendered me virtually catatonic. A year prior to dating Janet, I had been caught in flagrante by a very angry father. I never really recovered from the experience. In addition, I already had the awareness that most people find annoying. I am always standing a half pace back, observing myself and my friends with a detachment that earns me the adjective "heartless."

Janet was almost my polar opposite. She was naive and open to experience. There was a warmth to her character that charmed most people, and an earthy sensuality that excited most men and more than a few women.

Her parents, for reasons I found inscrutable, seemed to enjoy my presence. It was taken for granted that I would stay for dinner, if in the house after four o'clock. This was true even after Janet had left me for one of my friends. In later years I realized that her parents found my adolescent bewilderment infinitely preferable to the wet, knowing grin of my replacement. They identified something in Eddie that took me a few years to spot. He shared with Janet an ability to find the limelight. As with her, the last time I saw him was on the TV. He had been leading a street demo to defend the civil rights of a group of pornographers. It came out later that he owned one of the clubs threatened with closure.

I suppose that was why her parents called me when she entered the ashram. By rights it should have been Eddie there weeping with them. My relationship with Janet—notional at best—was long since over. But call me they did, incoherent on the phone. Fearing the worst, I rushed over. Their house reinforced my fears. It had the kind of disarray peculiar to violent mourning, the kind of mourning that happens when a child dies. Janet's father's eyes were red-rimmed and swollen, and he was at least half-drunk. He was a corporate lawyer, normally polished and controlled. The idea of his weeping unnerved me far more than his intoxication.

"How could she do this to me?" was his greeting.

Her mother, the source of Janet's beauty, appeared to have aged a decade since I last saw her. Her normally straight back was as bowed as if she had spent her life pulling turnips. "Do you know anyone else who was in on this?" she asked.

I realize now that it was her need for an answer to that question that made her plead with me to come over. I was there was to confirm Eddie's involvement. But dim as I was, I could not see Eddie getting involved in anything that had the faintest whiff of self-denial. And despite the later scandal, to join the ashram you shed your material possessions. Acolytes did, anyway.

In due course, attempts had been made to wrest Janet from the clutches of Hindu mysticism. They must have succeeded to some extent. When the ashram dissolved amid the usual claims of financial misdoing and sexual misconduct, Janet had emerged healthy and clear-eyed. She even directed a documentary about it.

She appeared suddenly before me, as if my thoughts had summoned her. "Phil! You have not aged a bit!" she said with a brilliant smile. "Not like me." Her arm described a graceful arc that encompassed her whole body. That she was stout should not have surprised me, given the lush curves of her youth, but I had foolishly expected the old Janet, forever young, forever beautiful.

Her beauty was still apparent through the extra weight. Her cheekbones were still defined, her features symmetric. Her liquid eyes, always attractive, were outlined with kohl. Her lips were still full, made noticeable with a bright red lipstick. Even the grey in her hair somehow seemed glamorous. Despite her weight, despite her cheap polyester sari, she looked marvellous.

She perched herself on the edge of the wicker chair. It was a child's pose: bum barely on the seat; her feet, shod in the cheapest of Indian flip-flops, tucked under the chair, ready to launch her like a stone from a sling. The waiter gave her an avuncular smile, which she returned warmly.

"A mangohattan?" he asked.

"Please!"

"Another gin," I shouted to his back.

"So," she said. "You are a success!"

I had to suppress a simper. It was shocking, but even after all these years she could still work her magic on me. "How on earth did you know I was in India?" I asked. When she had identified herself on my GSM, I had been shocked into incoherence. The last time we spoke, cellular phones had not existed. Or if they had, we were not impressed by them. Mind you, in those days we were trying desperately not to be impressed by anything.

"My mother of course," she said. "She ran into your father, back home, in the supermarket."

My father, god bless him, would give out my number to anyone. "Your parents still live in Winnipeg too then?" She nodded.

We sat and stared at each other. I was horrified to find I had absolutely nothing to say. What does a middle-aged business consultant say to a middle-aged mystic? "So... are you in another ashram?"

Another laugh trilled. "Oh no. I left that behind long ago. Did not you see my documentary?"

I had in fact. During my first supervisory assignment, I had been living in a low-rise motel on the outskirts of Des Moines. It had been a brutal, lonely winter. I had been coming to terms with promotion, with the loss of the camaraderie of co-workers, and with learning how to extract performance from people. My fear of making mistakes had caused me to put in twice as many hours as I should have done. When I hadn't been working I had watched TV or gone jogging, thumping through the industrial park where my motel was located.

Janet had appeared one night on my television, in the same magical manner she had suddenly appeared on my cellular. I had been flipping the channel and—there she was! She was narrating a documentary about the dissolved ashram. I watched the show until her matter-of-fact description of sex in the ashram. Apparently, frequent, public, and noisy congress was considered healthy. Her description and my memories were too much. I laced on my runners and headed out into the January night. That documentary had given me a case of laryngitis that had lasted nearly two months.

"But why India?" I asked. I noticed she now had the slightest of Indian inflections in her speech, an accent that had once been the purest Canadian.

She shrugged, sipped at the punch bowl of fruit slush that was her drink. And then looked at the stage. "It is home now."

I groped about, wracking my brains for any topic of conversation. "Are you married then?" I asked.

She shook her head. Her face had taken on the blank look you get from junior employees fearing for their jobs. "You?"

"Divorced."

Another trill of laughter. "So! I am out with an eligible bachelor!"

I smiled, although I suspect my tension showed. Was this to be a date then? Was I expected to take her back to my hotel?

She smiled at the waiter across the room. Within seconds he was at her side. "Another Madam?"

"Please. And a drink for my friend."

"A gin!" I shouted again to his retreating back.

She turned back to me and the warmth she had shown the waiter disappeared. She stared at me for a moment with that blank face. "Any children?" she asked.

"No. None."

We sat for a few minutes in silence, staring at each other. I had nothing else to say. Two decades earlier—hell, even one decade earlier—I would have found it inconceivable that I could be bored by Janet. Now I found myself thinking that if I made it to the airport before midnight, I could catch an earlier flight.

Two mangohattans appeared on our table. They were huge glasses filled with mango pulp and grenadine. "Hey!" I yelled at the waiter's back.

"Try it. You might like it," Janet said.

I sipped at it cautiously. It was sweet, the slightly chemical aftertaste of the mango brought forward by what I thought was over-proof white rum.

"You are still too conservative. You never were open to experience." Janet looked at the band starting to tune up. "I have one," she said.

"One what?" I asked.

"Child!" she said. "A boy. That is him. There. With the guitar."

As if that were a cue, the band began to play an American R and B tune. The lead guitarist, the boy whose beauty I had noticed earlier, was riffing. To my surprise he was more than beautiful. He was a very good guitarist.

I made a few compliments, but I couldn't talk over the band. And Janet was rapt, watching the band with shining eyes, leaning forward in her chair with her lips parted and her hands in her lap, her shoulders dipping slightly to the beat, her heavy bosom rolling in time.

When their set ended, with an unnecessary but impressive flamenco riff by her son, she turned to me and said "Do you think he is good enough for America?"

It was my turn to shrug. "It's a tough business," I said. I played with my drink, keeping my eyes away from her.

"I want him to leave India."

"What?" I said, looking up. Janet was looking at me very solemnly. "I want you to take him with you," she said.

"What?"

"You must! This country is no good! I want him to be free, to have the opportunities I once had."

"But you came here," I said.

"Please! You can afford it. Buy a ticket and take him away!"

The mention of money was pure Janet. Or maybe Eddie. I couldn't remember any more. "But what about your parents?" I said. Her father could probably buy my entire portfolio with one month's dividends.

"They do not know. How can I tell them?"

"They don't know you have a twenty-year-old son?"

"Twenty-two," she said.

"They'll take you back, Janet. You're still their daughter."

Janet sucked her mangohattan dry, and waved imperiously to the waiter. I pushed mine across the table to her.

"Would they?" She asked, looking toward the now empty stage. She turned and looked at me directly, her dark eyes sombre. "Would they take Raj?"

I was shocked. I had never thought of her parents as racists.

"And, anyway, I do not want to hear it anymore! I am tired of apologizing. I am tired of saying sorry-sorry for entering the ashram, sorry-sorry for fucking so-and-so."

It had all happened so long ago. I had been too young to realize that her family suffered the same problems all families suffer, that her perfect parents made their beautiful daughter feel wrong, that a pregnancy by an Indian was a mistake.

I could suddenly chart the entire arc of Janet's life. She had doubtless abandoned the child when she left the ashram, and then either been called or come on her own to reclaim him. And somehow her twenty-year-old embarrassment over the pregnancy had never been faced. But India is nothing like Canada. Could she explain that she was no longer thin? Her mother had kept her figure at least into her fifties. Could she explain the dirty feet shod in plastic flip-flops? Judging by her clothing it was a

87

good bet that her apartment would be condemned back home.

"You are the only one of my boyfriends they ever approved of, you know," she said.

She eyed me after saying this, with no apparent regard. There was a flicker of something across her face. Impatience maybe? It was gone too quickly for me be sure. "Does our past not mean anything to you?" she asked.

"Our past is rather past Janet," I said. "But why? Why do you want him to go?"

"Because of this!" she said picking up my drink and slopping some on the table.

"A mangohattan?"

"Yes! I want him to have a real manhattan, not some tropical fraud. And see LA. And buy real clothes. And have a dishwasher!" Her speech was fast. As she picked up speed, her voice began to singsong, the linguistic rhythm of Southern India. "You can do this. I know you can."

She tilted her head, and swallowed my drink, licking her lips. The alcohol had flushed her face, and the gesture was somehow lascivious. She leaned forward, and placed a hand over mine. "Oh where is the tender heart that I remember."

I shouldn't have been surprised when she said that.

Anywhere in the Western world, I would have laughed at such a statement. But in India you hear sentences like that all the time. There is a recognition of emotion, of matters of the heart here. When she had said those words, I knew that there was no going back. Janet had become Indian.

I managed to gather myself together and answer her. "Janet. I can't. He needs visas and passports and a place to stay, and all the things I can't get for him."

"You could adopt him! He could be yours you know. How do you know he is not?"

"Janet, for heaven's sake. He's Indian. He's twenty-two years old, and I haven't seen you in twenty-five.

"What about his father?" I asked.

"His father has a new ashram. And he cares nothing for music. He wants Raj to become a yogi. It pays better than music."

I could only stare at her.

"Oh...." She stopped whatever it was she was going to say, and turned to look at the stage. The band was back checking their tuning before the next set. "You are no good," she whispered. "You are no good," she repeated, louder this time. "You are just like my father."

There wasn't anything left to say. I stood up. "I have to go. I have a plane to catch." I pulled out my billfold and put all my American money on the table: four twenties, a ten, a five and a handful of ones. "Would you mind settling up for me. This should cover it."

She picked up the money, carefully smoothing the bills, exhibiting the regard for cash you only find in the poor. Then she tilted her head, proffering a cheek for a kiss.

I could still taste the wet salt of her tears on my lips as I walked through the doors of the airport.

Pancho and Gary
Angelo Eidse

For some reason incomprehensible to him, Pancho Bargen's mother made him stay in school even though he was already sixteen and more of a man than anyone in his grade-nine class; hell, he was more of a man than anyone in the entire school, including the principal.

One of the first things Pancho had to do when his family came to Grainview, a farming community of some consequence in southern Manitoba, was to take a stupid test to determine his placing in the school. They had put him back two years. He towered over his grade-nine classmates with their pale skin and pretty hair, their silky hands and soft bellies. Pancho's skin had the sun-blistered look of his father's, his hands were scarred, his knuckles hard. He had left his pinkie and most of the ring finger of his left hand on his uncle's cattle ranch in Chihuahua, buried next to a post of the barbed-wire fence that had taken them during an accident involving an angry bull and a pair of fencing pliers.

Pancho had twice failed the road test for his driver's license. It wasn't that he didn't know how to drive or that his nerves were bad, as was the case with many of his schoolmates; it was that he had been driving since he was nine years old, that he had learned to drive in Mexico on the back roads and fields surrounding Campo #24 and in the constricted streets of Chihuahua City in his early teens, and that the only instructions from his dad had been to drive in the spaces between the other cars, to try not to hit any people or cattle, but not to risk a wreck to miss a dog or chicken. On those trips into the city his dad had slouched back against the passenger side door with his feet up on the dash and his hat down, only his wide tobacco-stained grin visible. His dad seemed to relish the possibility of imminent disaster, and, instead of scolding his son on a near miss, would burst into laughter and kick the metal dashboard with the heels of his hand-tooled Tony Lama boots.

In the "Further Comments" section at the bottom of the road-test checklist, Pancho's driving instructor had characterized his command of his father's '78 Ford pickup as "unnecessarily violent."

Hank Bargen, Pancho's father, returned to southern Manitoba in 1985 after having spent thirty-five years in the Mennonite colonies in Mexico near the San Antonio Valley just west of Chihuahua City. Pancho's grandfather had packed his young wife and family (including three-year-old Hank) into a pickup truck, and had driven them south across the States and into Mexico at the height of Canadian nationalism following the Second World War, in fear of the growing modernization of society, the decaying morals of the church, and in the vainglorious hope of finally finding a place were they would be able to live out their Mennonite faith uncorrupted by vice and wealth and unmolested by governments.

Pancho didn't know much about his family history, nor could he have cared less if he had. All he did know was that they had driven north for days on end, his father cracking sunflower seeds to stay awake, to reach Canada where there was snow in the winter. (This had been used by his parents as an incentive to his younger brother and sister who were sad to be leaving their friends.)

Over a generation the Bargen blood had thinned in response to the oppressive, dry heat, leaving them maladjusted for the interminable Manitoba winters. Pancho would never forget the first snow he had seen falling from the sky in hollow chunks; like manna, only colder. It was Halloween night, he was fifteen, they had been in Canada for a month, and it had thrilled him; the pain of the sharp air seemed to be cleaning out the dust from his lungs. His younger brother and sister had pretended to be smoking cigarettes, bringing their fingers to their lips and exhaling clouds of smoke in the frigid air.

By the middle of December Pancho wondered if the snow would ever go away, and had he known it would last well into April, he would have complained less. What had shocked him the most was that people went out in it. They played soccer in it! He watched somewhat sadly as his younger brother Peter, who was just 13, squandered his superior soccer skills during noon-hour junior high intramurals, post-holing through shin-deep snow which had drifted onto sections of the soccer field. No one here knew how to play soccer worth a damn in the first place, snow or no snow. It was hard to believe, but these kids didn't place any real value on soccer. Volleyball was the thing—a bunch of kids separated by a fence, or net or whatever, bouncing the ball back and forth. Pancho thought it was a game better suited to children, and couldn't keep himself from blushing when forced to play it clad in his cut-off blue jeans during gym class. Occasionally (and for some reason he couldn't stop himself from doing it), he would punch the ball on a serve return, sending it careening off into the bleachers or crashing into the ceiling.

In addition to his lack of volleyball skill, Pancho was ridiculed for his broken English, which was heavily affected by his other two tongues, Low German and Spanish, both of which he was fluent in. He did poorly at his French lessons.

Pancho's mother, who was mestizo, being of Spanish and mixed indigenous blood, had named him after Francisco "Pancho" Villa, the bandit-cum-revolutionary hero who had been born in her village and was widely rumoured to have been her (along with most of the children born in her era) grandfather.

The name, which had earned the affection of many a man, woman and child in Mexico, in Canada only induced scorn and ridicule. Everyone took it to mean the ponchos women had worn in the late '70s, a fringed smock that looked ridiculous in backyard Kodachrome photographs.

"Hey Pancho, where's your poncho?"

If Pancho had known that the true source of the mockery he endured from his classmates was fear, he might have been able to take pity on them. Instead he held them in contempt, but performed for them by showcasing his awful strength and brutal physical resilience in the vain hope that he would be able to do something so extraordinary that they would champion him.

During Home Economics class, he had sucked back an entire bottle of Tabasco sauce (which he found relatively mild) without so much as a glass of water for a chaser. He did back-flips off of the monkey bars in the school playground, nearly breaking his tailbone in one failed attempt from the low roof of the elementary wing. He punched a hole in a classroom wall without breaking the skin on his knuckles. His classmates roared approval but turned him in, pulling down the poster he had hastily taped over the hole when the teacher came in from lunch.

Pancho would follow these acts of bravado and foolishness with a derisive shrug of his hefty shoulders. He became that rare kind of a hero who is, in fact, more of a spectacle; like some rare wild beast in a cage, no one wanted to get too close to him for fear of injury.

At some point Grainview school principal, Gary Loewen, an enormous man with flat feet who suffered with lumbago, had given up calling Pancho's parents. He had become exasperated at trying to explain the seriousness of the current offense to his father, or attempting to communicate anything at all to his often-hysterical mother, whose English was unintelligible. Instead he had devised a new strategy, one that weak-minded school principals and teachers often adopt: to make it easier for Pancho to drop out than to complete high school. This clearly went against an educator's general code of ethics, but it was inevitable at any rate. The kid had dropout written all over him.

"Just what is this?" the Principal asked Pancho. He balanced an Olympia beer can on the edge of his expansive grey desk. It had been crushed, and someone had gone to great lengths in the attempt to straighten it.

"Is that a trick question?" said Pancho with a smirk growing at the edges of his mouth. He sat in a hard vinyl chair next to the door of the cramped Principal's Office, which perpetually smelled of Rub A5-35.

"Don't get smart all of the sudden. You know what I mean."

"Well, Gary, I would say: beer can."

The Principal straightened his posture and adjusted his Obus Forme lumbar support. "Mr. Loewen," he said peevishly.

"It's a beer can, Mr. Loewen." Pancho rose to his feet. "Glad I could help you out. Let me know if there is anything else you ever need."

"Sit down!" The Principal rose to his feet, flinching as he straightened his back and pain shot down his sciatic nerve making his pinkie-toe twitch inside his size 13 brogue.

Pancho sat down. The Principal towered over him. Pancho resisted the temptation to poke him in the spare tire.

"Do you know who found this beer can?"

Pancho shrugged. He didn't know.

"Mr. Enns."

"Who's that?"

"The janitor, you...!" The Principal took a deep breath to a three-count. He put his hands in the small of his back and kneaded the muscles above his hips. Back in his day it would have been perfectly justifiable to, to what? Spank him? It was too bizarre to think about. Pancho would probably laugh it off anyway. This kid needed a bust across the chops, that's what he needed. No.

"The janitor, Mr. Enns," the Principal continued, "found this beer can in the lunchroom garbage. I've done some asking around. No one seems to know where the can came from."

This was new, thought Pancho. He had been giving Gary the run around because he thought that his classmates had ratted him out, as usual, and that this interrogation was mere theatrics. He had snuck the beer from his dad's supply in the garage fridge that morning before catching the bus, and had nonchalantly sipped it during lunch hour in another wildcard attempt to win acceptance. He had offered a swig of it to his nemesis Lorne Friesen, a swaggering senior, who had declined with a look of awe before checking over his shoulder for the lunchroom monitor.

"Mr. Enns digs around in garbage?" Pancho looked at the can, which had leaked a bit through a crack in the aluminum on to the Principal's grey desk.

"That," said the Principal, exhaling through his flared nostrils, "is not the point. The point is we can't have students drinking beer in school, or anywhere else for that matter."

"Why not?"

"Because!" Gary Loewen hated to hear himself say that as he prided himself a reasoning, logical man. "Because, you're a minor. Minors can't drink beer."

"How old do you have to get until you're a major?"

"What?"

"How old do you have to be before you can drink beer in school?"

"You can't ever drink beer in school you idiot!" It was too much and Gary knew it the second the words left his lips. "Sorry, I'm…"

Gary looked up and saw that Pancho had him. It was too easy. His back was torturing him; the nerves of his spinal column felt like they were being plucked like banjo strings. He had one course left and, against his better judgment, he leaned over and said, "Breathe in my face."

Pancho burst out laughing. He stood up. His wiry brown mop of hair only came up to the Principal's collarbone. He looked the Principal in the eye.

"Make me."

The Principal glared down into the wet blue of Pancho Bargen's eyes and knew he was defeated. His mind reeled backward as the pain in his back flooded his body with some despairing chemical. He had made bad decisions, he had let his distaste for this ignorant tuff derail his judgment. He had played right into the hands of a sixteen-year-old "Mexi." He felt himself blush. As was his habit when his nerves failed, Principal Gary Loewen began to chew on the inside corner of his mouth.

Pancho turned toward the door.

"Maybe I ought to go home for the rest of the day," he said over his shoulder.

"Yeah, fine."

"Better luck next time, Mr. Loewen." Pancho left the office door ajar.

Gary pushed the door closed, took a bottle of Advil from his desk drawer, popped three and lay down on the floor. The cool tile felt good through the thin fabric of his shirt. He loosened his tie.

"Next time."

Welcome to Mill Street
Cecilia Kennedy

"**Y**ou get off that road this instant!" Dilys from
next door screamed out the window of her
car at the boys who'd taken up the road for their
hockey game. The goalie with the Cardinal Red
Plumbing jacket dragged his net to the curb but she
wasn't appeased. Her dyed blond puff of hair hung
half out the window and her voice scratched up and
down Mill Street.

"Take up the whole road and can't be troubled to
move. In my day you'd 'a had your backsides
tanned. You brats don't even live on this street!"

I stopped raking leaves to listen, certain they'd
give her a blast of foul mouth for her pains. But the
boys just stood and waited for the old bat to get over
it. It was true they all lived around the corner on
busier Franklin Street so maybe they did feel out of
territory.

When Dilys finally ran out of steam she gunned
the old Valiant and lurched through the play zone
and onto my driveway. The boys charged back out
into the street, but, since her house is right beside
mine and she clearly had something to say, I could-
n't just go back to the leaves. I had to listen to more
Dilys Bryant views of the world.

She started by sniffing at my new old-lady hair cut. "You've had your hair done. And those are new slacks too." Not that she said she liked either my honest grey hair or the corduroys. In spite of her advanced age Dilys wore tight black leggings and strappy gold shoes you'd never rake your leaves in.

Then she told me that dead Arthur Thompson's house had been sold.

The news vexed her; it thinned her mouth, deepened the lines around her eyes. "You know who's movin' in there, Hannah?" Her sharp chin jutted toward the forty-year-old brick house with the sun porch I'd coveted for years.

"Who, Dilys?"

"You'll never believe it."

It mattered who lived that close. Our side of Mill Street was lucky enough to back onto the open lawns of Trefan Park. The side of my yard ran along a public walkway to the park, and on the other side was dead Arthur's house. It mattered who lived those ten feet from my kitchen window.

"It'll upset you, I know."

I pictured a family with eleven kids, seven teenagers. Hell's Angels. A Mormon with three wives.

"Get on with it, Dilys." I tried to sound a little dangerous.

"It was bound to come sometime. Those new subdivisions are full of them."

"My hands are starting to twitch. If you don't spit it out now I may never find out."

So she leaned close, confidential, like the trees might pass the word: "It's one of those, you know, Sikh people."

Mill Street never had much prejudice. Most I can remember was back in the sixties when Jim Poole used to stand on the stoop in his undershirt and holler to his boys that they better not be playing with those damned Delaneys. That was so stupid and so long ago I probably have to explain that the Delaneys were Catholic and Jim Poole marched in the Orange parade.

So when Dilys leaned close to confide that the fellow wore one of those, you know, turban things, I backed up. It doesn't matter to me what he's got on his head, I thought.

"He." A single man then. That sounded all right.

"Just one man came to look, but he'll likely have relatives with him and he'll rent the basement to more," she said, like she'd read my mind. Her head swung with deep sympathy. "And your kitchen, facing that way. You'll never smell anything but curry."

"I've always been partial to a nice curry," I said and started up the leaf mulcher so whatever she was going to say next was drowned out by the most satisfying roar.

"That woman's narrower than hen's eyes." It was nice to hear the clear echo of my husband's voice. Dead five years, Harold used to say that about Dilys Bryant at least once a week. Still, I couldn't help a little stir of apprehension about the multitude of relatives she'd conjured up. Things would be different on Mill Street and different things were not, at age seventy-two, my cup of tea.

However, when the new man moved in he turned out to be just one man. Late fifties. I got a good look at his furniture as the movers carried it in and it seemed like it could have come from Sears or The Bay. He stood in the yard wearing jeans and a T-shirt, his face harried like the faces of most people on moving day. Yes, there was a turban on his head, a light sage green, but it wasn't a really big turban.

One box of dishes fell with a frightful smash and I started thinking back to the last new people on the street (Robinsons, number fifty-two) and how I made them brownies and Dilys, not to be outdone, did a cheesecake. For the first few days a parade of baskets and gingham cloths streamed to their house, coming away with bits of news about where they were from (Winnipeg), why they'd moved (transfer), and what the wife did for a sideline (piano lessons).

Right away I knew there wouldn't be any such parade to the new neighbour.

"So you do it," said Harold. A union man, he always was for the underdog.

I'd rather have not. I like things certain and familiar. What could the new man know about such a small town tradition? He wouldn't know if no one came. Likely.

But Harold worried me and after two days I couldn't stand it anymore. I baked my plainest bran muffins with no raisins or nuts in case there was some food thing I didn't know about, and I chose my time carefully. Nine-thirty in the morning, kids off to school and mothers regrouped for coffee and newspaper.

Except for Dilys. Just as I stepped out the front door with my basket and that telltale splash of red checks, her door slapped open and out she came, fake fur coat half on, high heels clattering with the rush, and hot to know.

"What's wrong, Hannah?" The concern in her voice was real. "Is Josie in hospital again?"

All summer the street pulled together for Josie Kozak, three little kids and chemotherapy to go through. Babysitting, cooked meals, grass cut; Mill Street did it's best for them.

I looked straight at her and said, "I'm just on my way to welcome the new neighbour."

"Oh." Her mouth formed a perfect lipstick circle, held the pose for an hour and then she finally reverted to being Dilys and giggled, "So tell me what he's like, eh? You know me, I got to have all the news."

He was very shy. Also very polite.

"Welcome to Mill Street. I'm Hannah McBride from next door," I said as I pushed the basket in his direction.

"Thank you." He took the muffins with a smile that wrinkled up the corners of his eyes. Then he bowed.

How do you answer a bow?

"That is very kind. I am Harkamal Singh." He bowed again. I remembered that all those people have the same name.

"You live across the walkway?" he asked. "I admire this garden. The striped leaf plants, what are they?"

"Hostas." I said. His voice sang up and down in a pleasant, perfectly intelligible way. He said Mill Street appealed to him because of the gardens, the old houses and the big trees. For Dilys' sake I found out that he was a retired teacher, his wife had died and his children were grown. So much for the basement full of relatives.

But I never got around to telling Dilys because that was the night the first eggs landed on my house.

"You poor dear," she said the next morning as we stood in the backyard surveying the mess. Long streaks of white dribbled down the brick, set here and there with bits of yolk and shell hardening in the glaze. The back of the house had been attacked from the park, something I'd heard happened out there in the wicked world, but never before on Mill Street. Never to me.

"Halloween," said Dilys. "They ought to be horsewhipped."

"Its just eggs," I said, contradicting her out of habit. Inside I felt a little nauseous at the smell of raw eggs drying in the sun. Slightly sick at the thought of lying asleep in my bed while the hard shells cracked on the wall outside my room.

"Well I'd get it off before the sun baked it hard.," said Dilys, and left.

I was scrubbing away with an old brush when the new neighbour appeared in his back yard. Across two fences and ten feet of walkway he asked what I was doing.

"I've been egged."

"Egged?" Today's turban was a peach shade. A deep frown settled around his eyes.

"It's just a prank kids play around Halloween. You know about Halloween?"

"Yes." he said, curtly. Offended, I thought. I felt like I'd said "look" to a blind man.

For a minute he just stood there, looking sombre. Like he might have made a mistake buying in a neighbourhood where the houses of widow ladies get egged. "Why would they choose your house?"

"Search me," I said and stopped scrubbing long enough to consider the openings along the fence that might make me a good target. Or provide cover for an ambush. But there was nothing that made my brown brick house, in the middle of a row of seven, stand out any more or less that any of the others that backed on to the park.

"Just unlucky," I said.

He spent the next hour helping me scrape the bits of shell off the rough brick and even brought over a ladder so he could reach the higher bits.

When I met Dilys by the meat counter at Loblaws I told her how helpful he'd been, thinking she might come round to him, but she'd got a completely different notion in her head.

"Well that's as it should be!" She slipped her buggy up close and said, "Who do you think those eggs were meant for?"

I just looked at her.

The next morning the house was plastered again and she leaned over the fence and said, "You ought to put up some sort of sign. No turbans here. With a big arrow pointing toward his house."

"That's not one bit funny, Dilys."

There was another morning gone, scrubbing off the back wall. Again Mr. Singh came over to help.

The sun of the last few days had disappeared and it was cold work with the wet brush. After an hour I said, "Maybe I should just leave it? They'll come back, see it's already been done and move on."

"If I caught them I would make them lick the walls," he said.

That sounded like something from Harold's mouth, except that with Harold I'd always known such talk was pure hot steam. Mr. Singh with his blazing dark eyes was harder to read.

But when we talked about garden plants and the difficulties he'd face next spring with the amount of shade in his yard I got to know him quite well and decided that he would make a comfortable neighbour after all.

That night I sat up and watched the harvest moon, round as a white plate, move across the night sky. Most of the leaves were gone now and from the unlit kitchen I could see clearly into the park. Just kids, school night, I thought they'd be around sometime before midnight and I was right.

They came from the south where the cars of Franklin Street lit the field in passing streaks. Three dark shapes moved between bare branches of dogwood, disappeared behind Dilys' cedars, reappeared at the gap between my purple sandcherry and the Rose of Sharon. Then the first splat hit the wall.

Out the front door I went and down to the walkway. The light from Mr. Singh's kitchen, a golden yellow bit of warmth on the dark path made me wonder what I was doing, prowling around the night after some silly boys.

I had no plan. I think I just wanted to see who it was wasting so many of my October mornings. If they'd been big or frightening likely I'd just have crept back along the park fence and home.

That would have been easy enough, they were so engrossed in the joy of the game, lobbing one egg after another at my house, giggling and jeering at the missed shots with covered laughter. Only three of them, and in the moonlight I recognized the Cardinal Red jacket of the goalie from Franklin Street. Then I tripped over a branch and crashed right into the middle of them.

"You alright?" Red Jacket said after a long stunned silence.

"I'm fine." I said and then a hand reached down, hauled me up and I was standing beside Mr. Singh who looked rather frightening in the gloom.

"What have you done to this lady?" he said, his swarthy eyebrows knit tight and his beard black as a pirate.

"Nothing," said the three boys together. I was surprised they didn't run. "She was just walking and she fell. It's kind 'a dark out here."

"Why are you throwing eggs at her house?" He had a way of moving his shoulders that made them look twice as big, and his voice was deep and rasping.

"Her house?" The boy with the red jacket looked at me, aghast, then at the other two, then at my brown bricks already crusted with broken shells. "That's your house?"

I nodded.

"We didn't...we thought...I mean..."

They looked at me and at Mr. Singh and suddenly I didn't want to hear what came next.

"Who were you thinking of?" asked my new neighbour, his voice quiet with sadness and defeat and I knew after all that he wasn't the kind who would make them lick the bricks.

Red Jacket looked down at his cartons of Canada Grade A Eggs, Large.

"It's that battle-axe with the gold purse. The one who tries to run us down when we're playing hockey. We thought this was where she lived!"

The next morning we were already scrubbing when Dilys appeared in her silk housecoat.

"Dilys," I said. "This is our new neighbour, Mr. Harkamal Singh."

She had no choice but to shake his hand. Then she smiled sideways at me like we shared a secret joke and said to him, "It's so kind of you to help out! That's what I call the real spirit of Mill Street!"

"That woman's dumb as pullets," said Harold.

Mr. Singh bowed.

Principles
Frank Symons

We'd gather at Marty's Bar and natter like beavers at sundown.   Banter about getting sex at the table in a blind pig, joke about a club patron casually beaten unconscious and dumped in an alley for refusing to pay a gal's drink, lament a showgirl who lied to her pimp and turned up at the bottom of the St. Lawrence wearing cement shoes. Those were the days!   When I was young in Montreal in the 1950s.

If we'd had the money we'd have gone uptown to the El Morocco Club to sip Singapore Slings sparkling in the expanses of mirror. To float with the glitterati as they greedily sliced into filet mignons. To watch Lili St. Cyr hold court at her private table by the stage where Moke and Poke performed their "apache" dancing, feigning a lover's quarrel by tossing each other over their shoulders, then colliding in a forgiving embrace.

Instead we farted around at Marty's, our watering hole lurking behind the checkroom of a restaurant, dimly lit like a smoke-filled washroom.   We babbled. We coughed. We teased. We engaged in verbal swordplay beneath photos of Olympic gold medallists Bert Schneider and Lefty Gwynne, Canadian prizefighters.   Not for us the hard expensive

stuff—we drank affordable, skunky hops.   Sometimes Pop, a retired bouncer in the clubs, joined us.

I remember our conversations at Marty's in the
winter of 1953.   One afternoon during that winter,
heads turned to a gravelly Louis Armstrong kind of
voice, except the man was white.

"I saw Lili up close once, at Aldo's in the wee
hours" growled this voice belonging to Mackey of
the McGill Daily.   "What a satanically beautiful woman! High cheekbones, perfect dimensions, arched
eyebrows.   Up close I felt the mystery, the sin, the
animal in her, and, well, instant arousal. Her naked
undulations stay etched on my mind forever. She always told a story, like in her 'Suicide' act where her
lover jilts her and she's in the depths of despair.
Thinking of the guy made her writhe with desire as
her clothes fell away.   Suddenly she stood up on the
windowsill to jump. We shouted, 'No, Lili! Don't
jump!'"

"Yeah right," Fat Neck George said.   After years
of guzzling beer his throat was layered, like rings on
a tree.   "Look fellas, to her a man is an inferior spe-
cies.   To her, men are either clients or suckers."
Heads down, we sipped our liquid hops.

George continued, "Remember her show about
Salomé the biblical slut who asked for and got the
severed head of John the Baptist on a platter? Did it
the night before the 24th of June—St. Jean Baptiste
Day, the patron saint of Quebec.   So of course they
charged her. She asked for it...."

"She's free as a bird now," Gravelly Voice cut in.
"The prosecution's chief witness had never person-
ally seen Lili dance. Three housewives at the Gayety
Theatre witnessed her dance and testified they saw
nothing morally wrong. They said she retained her
bra and panties as she danced around the huge

apple in her 'Eve' number. Nobody testified she took her bra off in the end."

"Well, Lili St. Cyr plays her game and she wins every time. But what about Nancy Innis? Nancy played a riskier kind of game." Out of the corner of my eye I saw Fat Neck's elbow dig Gravelly Voice in the ribs. "You chased after your little Nancy in the jazz clubs, eh John."

"Oh yeah," I said, stiffening. Did Fat Neck smell my fear?

"Nancy's the opposite of Lili's tall statuesque figure and elegant style," Fatso, like a man with a knife, prodded. "Nancy is a delicate thin woman like say, Audrey Hepburn. She wears a belted trench coat all year round. She doesn't care about style yet she's totally feminine. Lili radiates feline power. Nancy radiates feline innocence."

I fought to keep the focus on Lili, away from my Nancy. "You've got it wrong George. Lili and Nancy aren't opposites. They both believe in their principles. In fact they live their lives according to their principles, black and white principles, no grays, no compromises, nothing in between. Like Lili once said, 'When you marry someone—or even when you establish an intimate liaison—you're responsible before all else to that person. I detest that situation because it's a vicious circle. The more I stay with X, the more responsible I feel towards him. My freedom is cut off. I'm not able to be myself any longer.' She's on rich husband number five now."

Gravelly Voice growled, "Lili also said, '... Sure I broke hearts and emptied pocketbooks. What's the point of being beautiful if you can't profit from it . . . What's the point of having money if you can't spend it?'"

Good, they're stuck on Lili. Pop piped up, "Lili once said, and I quote: 'Sometimes I feel romantic. One night in the El Morocco I saw a handsome foreigner, the kind of man you dream of meeting in a strange city, a man with a crude but irresistible charm. A massive hunk, a hint of menace, meanness in the shape of his lips. Forbidden fruit. The kind you dream of conquering but you're uncertain, not sure you can do it.'"

"So, Lili the predator, lured by forbidden fruit. What about Nancy the predator? What forbidden fruit did she hunt for before she met you?" George, like a German shepherd now, jaws clamped down on me. "I pay attention to the women who come to my office to work. Nancy worked for us briefly. I found out what she liked best."

"What's that, George?" Gravelly Voice asked.

"Her thing about the jigaboos."

"The what?"

"The coons, the black boys. You were right John, she goes for them, spends her nights in the Negro clubs," George said like he's purging, flushing something away.

"Look George, you've got it wrong again. I never said she went for black boys," I protested.

"You didn't, eh? Well, you could've fooled me, pal. When she worked in my office she couldn't concentrate, had a glazed look in her eyes. Hopped up with the coons making passes at her. Probably in bed with them, too."

"Just hang on there, George," I challenged. "You see things with your own eyes. You've got it wrong again. It's not like that at all."

"Fine. So how does she explain herself?"

I patiently told them Nancy's story about what happened to her when she was eight years old.   She had no siblings, no friends except classmates who lived too far away. Her mother died. Her father was indifferent to her. She got up the courage to talk to a black boy she'd spied swimming by himself. The boy later walked with her. He was her age. She felt like she'd just acquired a brother, so important to her in her heart because he was beautiful and this was her secret.

He took Nancy home to his folks who adopted her into their midst like she was family. She played that summer and the next with her beloved new mates. They were in rural Nova Scotia and her shopkeeper father didn't pay much attention. As long as she was home for supper he was happy. One day he told her: "I've got my reputation with my customers to think about. No more parties with the Negroes." Nancy cried for weeks. Her father was her only parent. She obeyed her father but her attitude towards him changed, turned covert, to a hidden hatred of everything he stood for.

That winter I kept dropping in to Marty's for a glass of ale and conversation. The topic of Nancy and her attraction to Negroes kept coming up. Usually it was George who started talking about Nancy again. One evening I think Gravelly Voice got fed up with this talk because he teased George with a chuckle, elbow into my ribs this time, "George, you're getting cynical in your old age." A mistake. He hadn't taken George seriously, plus he'd insulted him with the "old age" quip.

"I am not cynical on this issue, " George protested.

"Come on George, lots of white girls go for the coloured boys in this town," old Pop put in.

I decided to provoke George. "Only certain kinds of jobs are available to Negroes, like porters and shoe-shine boys," I said. "They can't get their share of jobs. They're in an economic ghetto. Nancy gravitates naturally to them. She needs the warmth of a family, people she loves. She wants to help them out."

"I hate this we-must-love–the-Negro stuff," George said. "Fundamentally it's harmful. What good is it going to do if people like Nancy come along and say, 'Everything I have is yours.'? Particularly if all she has to offer is one thing. I'm sure she's slept with God knows how many of them." This guy is repugnant, vicious, a real racist.

I'm not a violent person but I remember I wanted to fight him, verbally that is. Born and raised a Quaker in Toronto, I've an overwhelming sense of duty. One day I told George exactly that and he immediately asked, "Even when it's against your own interests?" "Especially then," I replied.

I had met Nancy a few months before this talk about her at Marty's. I remember well that first time I met her. She was sitting by herself in a plain white blouse and plain black skirt, in a Negro jazz club down in the St. Antoine district. The strange stillness of this lone white woman pulled me to her table that first time I saw her. We fell into conversation right away. I sat down and we talked until a Negro who knew her came over.

A week later I walked Nancy home for the first time to a stone house up the slope of Drummond Street. A small door at the street level. A room along a dark corridor. A narrow iron bed. A little shelf with an oilcloth curtain where she kept a few dishes. Mostly single women lived in this house, she said.

"Why did you come here?" she asked.

"Why did you let me come?" I asked.

"I like you. I sense you're a kind person," she said with a warm smile.

She made us a cup of coffee. "Ever noticed?" she asked. "In Montreal, people walk on rooftops. I've been up on the roof, seen them, strolling casually around brick chimneys and steel vents curved like periscopes. I've followed the small figures as they move across the sky, hands cupped over their eyes, scanning the horizon. I lift my hand and wave as if we've arranged to meet, and we're waiting, searchingly, on opposite street corners. No one ever waves back. We're all total strangers. This doesn't disturb me. Their presence comforts me. We're alone with our thoughts, we're independent."

I was hooked by her innocence, her waif-like demeanour. She was indeed a kind of Audrey Hepburn. I realized as she talked that I'm as alone in this city as she is, and that this fact makes her beautiful in a sense, in my eyes, the way a scar sometimes distinguishes rather than disfigures a face. I felt she'd given me a glimpse of something broken in her, and I decided I was in love with her.

We kept meeting as she told me more about her "family" back home, how eventually she stopped seeing black faces and frizzy hair and broad noses. She became aware of individual—not Negro—facial expressions, favourite words, songs, foods, and ideas. Her innate white reactions to Negroes fell away as she discovered the humanity of individual black people.

I was talking to a rare person. I liked that. I'd never met a person like her and I thought about her every day.

Meantime, I kept stopping at Marty's. I recall one time it was early March and there were drifts of heavy wet snow outside when Marty himself got into the usual conversation about Nancy. "Nancy picked my place last week to have a drink with a coon," Marty said. "Let's say she brings another one, then another, then another. Soon I'm running a nigger's bar and I could lose my license. Some of those nigger joints can't ever get a license. In no time I'm finished. I'm through. Finito!" He drew his finger across his throat, with a menacing scowl declaring, "I got to protect myself, you know what I mean?"

"Yeah, Nancy's got no tact, I see what you mean, Marty," said Gravelly Voice, nodding, unctuous, as if an oracle had spoken. What a bloody weasel!

I relayed this to Nancy. She bristled. "You can tell your friend Marty from me that my friends behave in his place. I behave too. He's got a license and he can't refuse to serve my friends and me. If he wants to keep his license he has to serve me whether he likes it or not."

Later during that month of March I let loose at Marty's. I declared, "Look here fellas, let's say Nancy's fascinated by Negroes the way white girls or white guys crave sex with exotic-coloured people. Then you could say she's perverted. But let's say she's attracted to them like ordinary white folks she's gotten to like. If I were a Negro she'd come to like, I'd be hurt if I couldn't be friends with her just because I'm coloured."

I lectured every week at McGill, but here I wondered, am I being naïve about their reactions? Their eyes studied me, curious. I kept talking. "If I had coloured friends and we liked each other then they'd tell me stories about how they'd been humiliated by whites. I'd feel guilty. Maybe what Nancy does is bad judgment. Maybe she shouldn't show so much sympathy for Negroes. Maybe it's her effort at being brave, facing up to intolerance. Injustice. Bigotry. You can't fault her for her bravery."

Silence. Even amongst the surrounding tables. Slowly the talk drifted to other topics. I felt miserable so I shuffled out, happy to get out of there. I trudged north through the dark underpass, past sounds of smashing glass from inside a club. Disillusion enveloped me like a cloud. I cursed my own Quaker goody-goody culture for making me abhor conflict. George, Marty, and even weasel-face Mackey hated Nancy. Their attitude became a poison spreading like a film of oil, brilliant and treacherous.

I figured what I lacked was information, so I dropped by Nancy's favourite jazz club, late. She wasn't there. I headed straight for the piano player I'd seen at Nancy's table many times. Fast Fingers Waldon was a tall thin man with a lined face. "I'm John Jackman," I said. "I'm a friend of Nancy's."

"Is that so? Now I think on it, I seen you at her table. A smart kid, pretty too." he said. It was his break and we sat down. I offered him a beer. He chose Dow's ale and so did I.

"She has a lot of sympathy for your people," I said.

"Yeah, a friend," he admitted. I felt him sizing me up, carefully. I figured no harm in talking about myself so I told him a little about my own background in Ontario. Then I asked him about Nancy.

"Quiet and like a little lady, that's the way she sits," he said, almost to himself. "Sweet and like a flower ready for someone to pluck. Don't dance, don't get drunk. Just here, like that, with us. But the brothers notice she's there, like she's waitin' for somethin'."

"She has sort of an innocence about her," I said.

"Lotsa white sisters come my way," he said. "It's figuring out what each one wants, that's the problem. Some are crazy about the music. Some full of class war and political conviction. Some want to experience a black man just once, or have an affair. It gets complicated. If the thing gets intimate the brother hides the old fear that if she squawks he's done for. It's white man's justice goin' to settle the matter."

He smiled, reflecting, unhurried. "Maybe Nancy just likes doing things by herself. Not that a girl can-'t do somethin' all by herself," and he grinned a wide grin. "Seriously now, I noticed somethin' about her innocent look. It's from her past. She's a country girl. Maybe Nancy don't realize black folks here in the clubs 'an in the big city aren't the same as black folks in the country where she's from."

"That's a salient observation, for sure," I said.

"Then Nancy came along and she gave me a wallop. I mean she was offering herself to me. But then I see her givin' the treatment to everybody, no good shoeshine boys, and lavatory attendants. I mean a low life is a low life in your race as in mine. That same easy affectionate way, an' I'm thinkin' he does-n't rate it but he gets the same treatment. You see?"

"Yeah," I said. I'm thinking this is not looking good.

"That's not it, though. What's happenin' is all us brothers are watchin' each other. White or black, guys are wise to each other. We don't trust each other when it comes to a girl. The devil inside gets to work. They's watchin' the whites who stop at her table, too. Like you."

"Yeah . . ." I mumbled.

"She treats our women the same as she treats the men. Only it works out different. You know what women are like. They get fat too quick, an' some don't do so good with their husbands and get sour. Soon the sisters see Nancy as a big threat an' they're hating Nancy's guts. They think they know what's goin' on."

He stopped, took a swig.

"You see the situation? The wives wanting to beat Nancy to a pulp. The brothers sittin' around suspicious, thinkin' bad thoughts, some thinkin' violence against each other. 'An Nancy she's from the country, hasn't a clue what's goin' down."

"Yeah, I understand," I said.

"Nancy sits there in her little white blouse," he said. "The brothers are drones around the queen bee. Sisters figure she's moving in on their territory. I stopped sitting at her table. Our band's our money, not much, but it's a living. I don't want no trouble. Some other brothers thinkin' the same, smellin' trouble."

"Yeah, trouble. I'm sure you don't want any trouble," I said, feeling sick. "I'd like to tell Nancy to stay away from here, but she'll stick to her guns, she'll say I'm the one who doesn't understand. Come to think of it, why don't you tell her yourself?"

"I don't want to offend. I can't insult a white sister when I've got nothing on her."

"This is awful," I barely whispered.

"If you speak to her, give me a little break brother, don't say I said anything. It would stir up the hate an' suspicion an' she's already stirred enough hate in this joint. I got to play again. Anything you want to hear?"

"No, nothing. Thanks for asking. Thanks for telling me about Nancy."

Head down, I trudged uptown in the slush, through the dark underpass. I thought about Nancy's white blouse and black skirt, her sudden smile giving her a glow, a country freshness. I figured she knew how she looked. She knew a man couldn't help wanting to reach out his fingers and touch her blouse and feel her soft flesh. It's not their fault the jazzmen want to sleep with her. It's their own male pride, scoring with a female. But I hated it, these guys going after her.

I trudged up Drummond to her little room. She made me identify myself before she opened the door. When she opened she turned away from me. I saw a small purple welt on her face.

"What's that on your face, Nancy? What happened?" I asked.

"A man stopped me in the corridor when I came out with some clothes for the dry cleaner's. He started talking about France where he'd learned a lot about tolerance. He went on about how a woman could have coloured lovers, how he could understand and be sympathetic to 'sophisticated people like you.' He tried to kiss me and when he saw I hated it, well, then everything changed."

"What do you mean?" I asked.

"I pushed him away. He pulled me towards him. He said, 'You sleep with those coons. They touch you and you like it. I touch you and you hate it. Am I such an animal to you?' His eyes glazed over, wild, and hurt. As if I was the one who had hit him. I wriggled my way down out of his arms, back into my room. Bruised my face against the door jam before I locked him out." I went out, bought her medicated cream, pondering—who was it? What do I really know?

It was snowing heavily for the third day straight, and the snow was deeper.

She put her hands on my shoulders to steady herself, as I applied the cream on her. The touch of her hands was gentle, her blue eyes tender, looking directly, openly at me. It was like she was silently expressing my importance to her. How good it was to talk to her, a natural refreshing person, not like those cynics down at Marty's. "If you don't see things the way other people do you're strange or pigheaded or stupid. Everybody's a friend as long as you conform," she said, staring straight into my eyes.

"You stick to your ideas," I responded. "If I may say so, this means you're thick-skinned. You won't allow yourself to be influenced." How was I going to tell her what Waldon said, the brothers watching like predatory hawks?

"You don't have to rub it in," she said.

"Nobody's saying there's anything wrong with you," I tried to backtrack.

"I won't be taken in by your high moral tone. You're thinking I live a kind of sleazy life. I know it!"

"It's not like that, " I said, noticing her white blouse and black skirt laid out on the bed. Sad, I sighed. "You're going down to the Negro jazz club," I commented.

"You know something, Frank?" she said. "I wish I didn't have a date. I wish I could stay here with you," she said, blinking. She seemed surprised she'd said what she did. "Anyway, you'll be around again, won't you?"

"Of course," I said.

"I like to keep my promises. I said I'd be there and I'll be there," she smiled at me. "You do understand that. I know you do." Should I go with her to the Negro club? She's in danger. She's got to stop going to those clubs. How do I tell her? How do I change her attitude about it?

I went home to bed without telling her about my talk with Waldon.

That same night I had two vivid nightmares. In the first I dreamt two tall Negroes walked up Nancy's street, one of them Fast Fingers Waldon. Dressed in black fedoras, black overcoats, silent like undertakers. They went straight to Nancy's and entered. "Nancy, you must leave town," Waldon said. "The sisters make dark threats but we're worried about their men."

"You worry too much," Nancy replied.

"Look here Miss Innis, the men don't talk but they're watching each other like hawks, watching to see who comes first to visit you," Waldon insisted. The big men leaned over her. "We don't want no fightin'." Then the men put their hats back on in unison. The man I didn't recognize said, "If things continue on this way Miss Innis, you'll be hearing from us again."

I awoke in a sweat, changed my pyjamas, fell asleep again and then had my second nightmare. This time Nancy's landlady walked down Nancy's corridor. She tapped on Nancy's door. "Nancy, Nancy, are you there?" she called. There was no answer so she entered with her own key. "Oh I'm so sorry to disturb you Nancy," she said, seeing Nancy in bed, asleep. Then she noticed Nancy was about to fall out of bed. She tiptoed into the room, seeing Nancy clearly now, in bed, uncovered, her blue eyes wide open, mouth agape, head twisted to one side, welts around her throat, her legs open.

I awoke into the real world from that nightmare and stared at the clock, pondering my dreams. That last dream was an omen. I had to do something. It was only midnight. I threw my coat and hat on and ran the blocks along Sherbrooke Street to Nancy's on Drummond.

A crowd gawked at the front of the ground floor of the old stone building. Policemen held them back. Two delivery boys watched. I grabbed the arm of the taller one. "What happened, son?" I asked him.

"A woman in there hanged," the boy said.

"Prob'ly raped too," the smaller boy whispered.

"Get off! You don't know what yer talkin' about! She had 'er clothes on," the taller one shot back.

"She was naked! The guy over there said she was. I heard 'im!" the smaller one retorted.

The policeman curtly brushed me off, telling us all to go home. I kept repeating to myself, I've lost her, she's gone forever. Tears flowing, dazed, I headed up Mount Royal. I thought she'd never come back. I'd never been so sad in my life. I could have, should have prevented this. Up and up I forced my body through the heavy mountain snow. Like the lake at the centre, I felt frozen, abandoned, tired, and sick. My survival instinct drove me down, down the mountain, into town. Yes, that seemed right. Warmer, lots of people. Were the clubs emptying? Like a zombie I staggered along some street, coat open and blackened with street slush. Images flashed onto my inner eye, images of the police barrier, the black undertakers. I barely saw the pedestrians, the lights. Going insane? Was I losing my mind?

I crashed into a woman and fell like a drunk into the snow bank. The woman recoiled in horror.

"My God, what have you done to yourself? You look like death warmed over, bloodshot eyes and all. Look at you—your coat's filthy, and are those your pyjamas? What on earth is going on?"

My eyes focused. "Nancy!" I whispered. "Nancy, you're alive. It wasn't you they killed! Look Nancy, there is something I gotta warn you about before it's too late. About, about . . . down in the clubs, they told me it's a bad situation. We've got to talk before it's too late . . .."

"Shush, shush, John," she gently quieted me "Later. There will be plenty of time to talk. You're shaking like a leaf. Right now we need to take you home to get you warm."

Home, I mused, leaning on her as we walked. Home, our home, Nancy's and mine. We were married a few months after that. Today, fifty years later, we still frequent the jazz clubs. With political correctness Marty now smiles deferentially when he serves his coloured customers. It's good for business.

Inca's Return
Cyril Dabydeen

Strange new sensations gripped him the moment he arrived, as everything seemed unreal. "I am here," he let out nevertheless. And it was because of what he'd been accustomed to, and would likely soon forget. "I'm indeed here," he echoed.

But another voice began telling him he wasn't.

"Inca, you're not." This whirred in his ears.

Now he was being greeted by an aunt, an uncle, other relatives, all who would take care of him in the new country. And did they want him now to feel he truly belonged here? Again they embraced him, and asked many questions at once.

Inca muttered under his breath, "I'm indeed here."

His Uncle Hari, like a pronouncement, said, "We're glad you've come, Inca." Inca figured he would now wear fancy clothes: silk vests, silk shirts and ties, dress-slacks, all he'd seen in glossy magazines and were now within his reach. He'd also drive in a fancy car and live in a posh house.

Other relatives watched him and also smiled.

Yes, listening to the radio, watching colour TV in his room. Inca no longer felt tired; the jet lag had suddenly disappeared. A rush of blood only now.

"You know, you're lucky to be here, Inca," his Auntie Iris muttered.

"Lucky?"

"Thousands would like to come here."

"Why don't they?" Inca looked at her.

Then, "It isn't easy," she said softly, but with an almost scolding tone. But for Inca new possibilities were all before him; and it stemmed from his years of dreaming of where he'd be one day in the new country. He closed his eyes, still thinking...now as the "other" place he left came back, like a great big wave. A shimmer of sun's rays too he saw, and the shape of large trees: the jamun, guava, and palm with sprawling branches. Leaves rustled as the trade winds blew. Nostalgia began eating at his insides.

Next fruits like the star apple, papaw, semitoo, all with the once-familiar aromas, came back and started to overwhelm him.

But now he was indeed here, as Inca rubbed his eyes. He looked at the relatives, each one; and one used the word "immigrant." Ah, who or what was an immigrant? Unconsciously, Inca scoffed. Those looking at him appeared beguiling too, didn't they?

Inca involuntarily looked up at the far sky, the plane in the air, and where he'd been not so long ago. Islands, all somewhere. Then close-up places too, as if he was unsure of where he really was.

More relatives fluttered around him, with their sometimes many voices, all speaking at once. Inca simply wanted to shut his mind off from them; it was odd how this feeling gripped him. And he preferred to dream, alone, of the faraway place he left behind when he was in his room.

Now what else did he think?

New images flashed into his mind, like a maelstrom.

His Auntie Iris exuded a heady perfume as she hailed him the next morning. Her cheeks rouged, lips red—and so unlike his mother with corrugated skin she was. "How you've grown, Inca," Auntie Iris said and laughed. Did he really grow...overnight?

Inca wanted to tell her what he'd been thinking. Must he? He also looked at the others, amidst the images of palm trees, mango, star apple, semitoo stirring in his mind. A fresh gust of familiar trade winds he inhaled, if only like wishful thinking. His rib cage expanded automatically.

He closed his eyes, trying to conjure up more.

"Inca, it's different here for you now," added his Auntie. "But you're still young, you will adapt."

"Will I?'

"Yes."

"But what if I don't?"

His Auntie didn't understand this; but she was prepared to humour him. She smiled indulgently.

Suddenly Inca wanted the old images to remain with him forever, as a humming noise he heard deep in his brain.

Later that day he travelled in a shiny new car with the relatives, all who seemed willing to show off "everything." And indeed a new place it was, all where he was in, with wide streets, large buildings, the shopping centres. Here too where everything seemed so clean, the lawns trim, even the creeks, small lakes he looked at seemed like scenes in a pic-ture-postcard.

Inca kept being amazed! Then he was driving the car himself, and making sudden turns: left, then right, as everything yet overwhelmed. It all felt so dizzying.

But unconsciously he also longed for narrow streets with gnarled branches hanging from trees, like rafters; there where people aimlessly sauntered, not briskly walked about.

"No, Inca...this way," his Uncle Hari said.

Other relatives also guided or cautioned him, but Inca pulled at the steering wheel, wanting to make a sudden right turn.

More insistent he was. To go there?

No...Inca!

Cars zoomed past on a wide street—and what a thrill!

Inca looked at splendid buildings, high-rise...sky-scrapers.

Mannequins seemed alive, as some even hailed him from the department stores! One actually nodded to him, he swore. What a strange place. The relatives laughed.

"Ah, Inca, what you see isn't always real."

"Not... real?"

More laughter from the others. Like reflex action, Inca again pulled at the steering wheel harder, wanting to turn into another side street where it wasn't bright with neon. It was just his curiosity, or something else. Guffaws, he heard. Inca wanted to close his eyes and dream of the old place still; but the images now seemed hard to sustain.

Yet he must try!

After a while the images no longer appeared.

Then Inca started keeping to himself, just to be able to conjure up the past, like one last effort... to conjure up all he'd left behind. Those images mustn't ever disappear, as if he feared himself disappearing. No!

Something...about himself, which he thought about more and more, young as he was. Ah, nothing must ever disappear.

Everyone around him now wondered what was the matter with Inca. "Oh, it's really nothing," one relative said.

"Are you sure?"

"Quite sure."

Yet they looked at him and were puzzled by his expression. His face changing colour at times; his manner, even perplexing.

Inca, well, only whirred loudly to himself, like a leitmotif.

"He's our Inca," said another relative with glee.

"Look at him, how he's changing; oh, how he's grown," another chirped. And did they wonder about the life he might have lived there?

"He will never go back there," fired another.

Never?

For days, weeks, Inca remained almost in a daze; he kept to his room, and he wasn't sure what was taking place, or what he was thinking after the initial exhilaration of being in a new country.

He was frightened, too, and at nights he stayed awake.

His thoughts festered...in this temperate land as it seemed to him with snow falling; and no one knew his deep, inner thoughts but maybe his Auntie and Uncle.

From time to time Inca also imagined an ocean, like a great big place...a big body of water, and he was somewhere in it. Waves kept beating...and he was in a small boat, as he slapped the water with bare hands... moving along, yet adrift. Where was he going? Didn't he want to get to shore?

Somewhere...an island, to be all alone, he wanted!

His Auntie Iris in the middle of the night came to him when he called out. "It's not what you think it is, Inca," she said.

He rubbed his eyes. "It isn't?"

"Maybe you will learn to like it here. The temperate..."

"Temperate?"

"It was the same when we first came. I still remember that first day, Inca," she said in a consoling tone.

Inca stared at his Auntie, not sure how to react.

Then it intrigued him that his Uncle Hari and Auntie Iris had indeed come from somewhere else, and might have had thoughts like his too. Did they really? His Uncle smiled. His Auntie did too.

Inca was left to himself to think things over, about adapting; and again he turned and tossed in bed, and mulled over the familiar images... the tropics, a world he'd indeed taken for granted when he lived there. Now he conjured up houses on stilts, one or two even walking along on a narrow road...with the ocean really not far away.

Was this possible? The imagination's pulse-beat it felt like, all that he conceived because of distance and memory...or another place.

How really far away? The sky he looked up at...how far away?

It was the same he'd imagined before coming to the new land.

Once more he tossed and turned, but this time he didn't call out.

And no one knew how he truly felt.

Waves again, as everything began to seem timeless. And more islands he contrived, as if they were never real.

Now where did he truly belong? Just where?

Waves started threatening the houses, including entire villages, and what if his own village were no more?

Inca wasn't sure what was coming over him. He closed his eyes, and tried not to imagine more. A hurricane came nevertheless, as stronger winds blew. A tornado also? Then it was as if the houses were running away, like mobile homes (one Inca had seen earlier on a large vehicle). He was shocked at what he thought.

In the dark when he opened his eyes again, shadows moved around him; and maybe he wasn't feeling well. Silently he called out for his Uncle and Auntie. But no one was around in the new place, in a new world...it seemed. His mother...where?

Louder he called, with a feeling of vertigo. What was the matter with him? Outside... as he looked from the window, there were vast spaces, sheer emptiness, despite cars moving fast. He quickly closed his eyes again.

How he twisted and turned, as more waves came, against the window itself. Real? Then he was back in some distant place that he'd been trying to give up on. Clouds moving in a somersault, with voices yet asking, "Where are you really?" Was it his mother's voice, though he'd trained himself not to think about her?

"Why did you leave us?" demanded others, old friends, other relatives, some poor or just bedraggled-looking. The voices sounded real.

"No," Inca tried closing his ears, yet he wanted to hear everything.

The waves came crashing down. "Why did you leave, Inca?"

Palm trees, shrubs, all asked in a shrill voice. "W-h-y?"

Suddenly Inca didn't want morning to come, as he broke out in a sweat. He got up and looked out the window...once more; and where was he? More fast cars, people hurrying.

Ah, maybe what he imagined...wasn't real.

Or he wasn't here at all?

What was coming over him? The mannequins moving, talking to him still from the shop windows.

No! "Yes, Inca...it's because you are here."

"But am I not really there?'

"You are here?"

"I want to go back."

"You can never."

He wasn't sure if the world was indeed changing around him. A vision of wide lakes, rivers and trees like the fir, maple, beech. Yet he yearned for the houses on stilts next to familiar palm trees, and then the ocean's waves came once more.

Silence, deafening.

A hand on his shoulder; it was his Uncle Hari.

"I too couldn't sleep, Inca," he said.

The grind of tires, wheels on asphalt. Dogs barking. An ass's head maybe lifted up as the animal brayed against the sunset. Vermilion and russet hues everywhere. Police cars, sirens wailing, people screaming. Murder was taking place, and Inca felt his body ache; his muscles, every limb, throbbed.

"I know you came here...thinking," his Uncle Hari said.

"Thinking?" Inca muttered, looking at his Uncle's face etched against the wall...the high nose, cheekbones. Immediately he wanted his Uncle to return to his room.

"It's a nice city this," his Uncle said. "You will make all sorts of new friends here."

"Will I?"

130

"Yes."

Later, he yet heard his Uncle muttering, "Poor boy, he will adjust."

His Auntie: "But it's taking a long time."

"It was the same with us, remember?"

"Oh, yes. But did I really take that long to adjust?" she snapped.

"Maybe it's because Inca's parents are not here."

Why aren't they? Inca clasped his hands to his ears to block out their words. He indeed wished he were somewhere else, if only it was hallucinatory. What was he really thinking?

Silence... of the closed room only, with humming noises.

Inca's heart talked, like a tape-recorder's sounds. He figured he belonged somewhere. More voices, then the sound of a pebble dropping into water. A guava fruit falling into it. A cashew nut next with a bird looking down at its own fixed expression.

He was being sucked into a deep whirlpool also, and going under.

"No!" he cried out. Next, "Oh, God, someone. Help me!"

But no one came.

His Auntie, Uncle...where were they?

More relatives surrounded him, one or two calling out, "Look, you're here now, Inca!" They chortled, laughed, all so enthusiastic.

But strangers they still were; even his Auntie and Uncle he now didn't fully recognize.

One relative sensing his mood rasped, "Forget the past, Inca."

"Eh?"

"You're here now, you must start a new life!" came like a command.

"New life?"

"Think that you are born anew." Were they becoming impatient with him?

"But...?"

Water again, and now he was at the bottom of a large pool, if not the ocean itself, as he desperately wanted to come to the surface.

Faces from above...looking down at him...some even snarling. Strangers' faces all? Faces of people whom he didn't recognize any longer! Including his Auntie and Uncle?

More voices, including childhood voices, he heard. Then seeds of large fruits being dropped into the water. A dream becoming a nightmare maybe.

Frantically he raised both hands to stop things coming down on him...and hitting him!

"I am here," he yelled back.

"No," he heard a reply.

"I am!"

"Inca, you've never been anywhere else."

Then laughter...everyone indeed laughing, including his Auntie and Uncle. Inca was confused, his mind in disarray, and he wished he wasn't here at all. Tropical sunshine he longed for...the kind he didn't feel anywhere here. The glaze, as the sun seemed to sparkle. What was he thinking?

A rainbow next, in the arc of sky, and the sun almost ready to tilt over. Evening clouds again, mostly moving in the west.

Not east?

Gradually Inca started despising everyone—all because he was still going down, with waves around him.

Voices again...and hands reached out to save him.

Then his mother and father he saw....truly? They with the relatives calling out to him, all wanting to save him. From what?

From returning to a place he might no longer recognize?

More familiar sounds, of his childhood. Palm trees swished as he opened his eyes wide, and yet kept struggling; he was having difficulty breathing now.

Would he die? Oddly, he was still making the turn he wanted in the car: he was still driving it, as his relatives wilfully steered. And what would his Uncle Hari say to him next?

Inca only tried to remember where he came from.

Could he ever return?

Then slowly he began surfacing in the large body of water, alone, and the relatives were waiting to greet him with open arms maybe.

A real welcoming he wanted, in the new place, in the new land.

His mother and father being here too? Sisters and brothers as well? All here, in the land of thousands of lakes and rivers.

He looked at his Uncle in the eye, as if seeing him for the first time. His Auntie, too; and they both smiled.

Coconut trees against zinc-covered houses he saw, no longer distantly. Wind wafted, the trade winds no less, with the aromatic smell of fruits yet tropical.

Not temperate?

Where was the snow?

Was it summer, weather that would last forever?

Inca thought it'd take years for him to get to know each relative, and their trying to know him too. Time, or a vast distance...and vistas indeed disappearing. And other places from a long time ago too...because it seemed he'd reached his final destination.

His own mother and father called out. Echoes. Just then his Auntie and Uncle again came into his room.

But Inca only wanted to be alone, as he tried his best to fall asleep...as if deliberately to avoid the busyness of people, fast cars, neon lights, loud music. Everything moved faster all the time.

The TV also, with its incessant images; and how the radio blared with the talk-show hosts being at it...as if bringing the entire world close up to him at once; and he was yet thinking of going under again, in the large body of water, the deep ocean no less.

It was how he wished it would be.

Yet everyone wanted to show him something new, something different. But Inca didn't want to see something new or different. What for? The mannequins gesticulated again, like actual figures, almost like his only friends. Really?

A new day and night, a new consciousness altogether it began to seem like in his reverie. Suddenly he began laughing to himself.

How he laughed, as the relatives took turns showing him...and being amazed at his reaction. And they too laughed, as they believed that he was adapting well!

His Uncle Hari and his Auntie Iris believed this most of all.

His parents too? Where were they actually? Not long dead, which was why he came here? Such a world now, with time shrinking, and he wasn't sleeping and having a nightmare anymore. He was just being himself; he tried—as a way of coping—as he heard the trade winds blow...and he wanted to tell everyone about it, and about the familiar smells, all more than the imaginary, that only he knew about.

It was also his memory, and something deeper, akin to instincts, that made him different from everyone else, it was said. His teachers also said the same, and they left him alone, because he was unique, they said. And others wanted to shout out to him, as he wanted to shout out back to them...like a silent scream, as his Auntie and Uncle sometimes talked about!

Then Inca laughed, and nodded to everyone, without saying a word; and such was his expression...because the ocean directed it all, he figured. And the palm trees waved encouragement...the trade winds hurled, all that he knew intimately since the day he was born because of what he carried deep inside him, which no one else knew. No one...nowhere, or anywhere else.

Swearing at the Queen
Radhika Sekar

"We recognise the many contributions that immigrants and refugees make to our country." So declared Judge Sylvie Carrier as she welcomed the "would be" citizens, gathered in the room to create the great Canadian mosaic.

The script had changed very little in twenty years and Madame Carrier, who had delivered it so many times before, knew it by heart. Nevertheless the ceremony never failed to move her. My speech is the final phase, the sacred initiation, if you will, in the sometimes long and convoluted process of immigration. Although only ceremonial, it would be her face that they would remember forever as the face of Canadian citizenship. She was the personage, who, on behalf of the Queen, granted them membership into this land of peace and opportunity.

Overwhelmed by the burden of the sovereignty that she represented, Madame Carrier paused to dab her eyes with a tissue from the box of Kleenex that the court clerk—the only non-ceremonial official present—had placed on the desk. After collecting herself, she peered down at the sea of hopeful expectant faces and nodded approvingly at a South Asian gentleman who seemed to be listening with rapt attention, before commencing with the French version of her address.

Dr. Hariharan Iyer—Harry to his friends—only seemed to be listening with rapt attention. In truth he'd switched his mind off sometime ago, when the judge began listing the seemingly endless advantages of Canadian citizenship. No mention of bloody taxes!

Sandwiched between a young Somali girl and a teary, middle-aged Italian woman who could not sit still, Harry, who'd already lived here some thirty odd years, felt out of place among the odd assortment of "would be" citizens seated around him. Gazing surreptitiously around him, he observed a youngish Chinese couple in the front row. A family of Sikhs, probably from Bhatinda (Punjab), occupied a full row behind him, and, but for a fellow in the back who was undeniably British, the others were either East European or from the Middle East.

At least I'm not the only one who put it off. The Italian woman had loquaciously informed him before the ceremony that, like him, she too had lived in Canada for over thirty years.

"I no see reason to change citizenship," she explained, her English still not fluent after all these years. "But now my husband get cancer and say it time to get our papers in order. He no want that I have problems for pension later."

A good enough reason as any to apply for citizenship.

Harry had immigrated to Canada in the 1970s. Only, he and Manju had not known then that they were emigrating, for they'd had every intention of returning to India after Harry's training. His parents had expected, no, demanded it! And he dutifully promised to return to care for them in their declining years. But the Canadian way suited them and they lingered on. Before they knew it, they had built a comfortable life in Ottawa and his father, who had long tired of demanding their immediate return, passed away. Harry's mother came to live with them and thoughts of returning to India were finally laid to rest.

Manju had obtained her citizenship decades ago. Frustrated at being stopped and questioned by every "bloody immigration officer from here to Timbuktu," she'd flung her Indian document on the table one day and announced her intentions. "I'm fed up with this, this, bhangi, pariah, passport. It's useless. I'm applying for citizenship so's I can get a decent passport."

"But aren't we going back?" Harry had asked, pointing out that India did not recognise dual citizenship.

"So what!" she retorted. "I'll reapply for Indian citizenship if and when we do go back."

Harry was shocked by her flip-flop attitude. It was too practical. So bloody un-patriotic. But Manju had retorted that while India may have been her janma bhumi, place of birth, Canada was the karma bhumi- the land of her karma.

At times, especially when was he singled out for extra attention at airports and border crossings, Harry had also considered applying for citizenship. But he vacillated in deference to his father who had been fiercely patriotic.

Finally, after September 11th, Manju took matters in hand.

"You fit the racial profile," she pointed out in her matter-of-fact way. "They're bound to check you at every airport—especially in the U.S. where they can't tell the difference between an Indian and an Iraqi. Look how they treated poor Rohinton Mistry!"

And with wifely concern for his welfare, she'd filled out the forms and even mailed them for him, after he'd signed them.

Thus he was here today. Waiting to swear allegiance to a British Queen and finally become a Canadian citizen. I'd rather swear at her. Not that he had anything personal against Her Majesty. The portrait on the wall showed a nice-enough lady. But his father had gone to jail to rid India of British Rule, and he felt he owed him some protest.

The Italian woman was fidgeting again. I know how she feels, thought Harry. Get on with it Madame Judge.

Actually, Pina Catrelli was not bored at all. In spite of herself she was impressed and moved by what the judge was saying. All said and done, Canada was a good country, and they had been very happy here. But right now she was worried about her Alphonso, sitting in the visitor's section. He had insisted on coming to the ceremony although she'd begged him to stay home and rest.

"No, my Pina," he'd said, his voice going husky like it did when he made love. "It's a memorable occasion and I wanna come see you swear to the Queen."

He had become a citizen decades ago. But Pina, who felt that her Italian identity was the last connection she had to her parents and her remote childhood, was reluctant to relinquish it.

As the Judge continued in French, Pina thought back to the day when Alphonso announced his decision to emigrate. He was twenty-three—so handsome, with a full head of dark curly hair and a confident swagger. She'd been only nineteen at the time and hesitant to leave the security of her family and village. But Alphonso promised that they'd return to Sorrento in southern Italy when they made their fortune.

It had been tough getting used to the different social environment and weather. But Canada in the '60s was booming and there were plenty of jobs available. Alphonso found steady work in construction and eventually started his own business.

"Little Berto will take over the business," he announced proudly, the day their son was born, "and we return and buy farm."

Business was successful; they prospered and settled into the social whirl of the large Italian community in Ottawa. "Canada is good country," Pina would say. "The people, they leave you alone." By people she meant Canadians. For as far as she was concerned, "us" would always be Italiano.

Now Alphonso was sick and she was becoming a citizen. "Cancer of the liver," the doctor had explained gravely. "It's quite advanced and he'll have to start treatment right away."

"Little Berto," who had shown no interest in construction and gone into accounting instead, advised her to apply for citizenship as soon as possible. "The political climate is unsteady," he said, in a husky voice so like his father's. "Immigration rules keep changing as more people apply to come here. The social welfare system, especially OHIP, is also strained to its limits and who knows what will happen. It's best you apply for citizenship at once or things may get complicated later on."

So she had applied and now six months later was here to swear at the English Queen whose portrait hung on the wall and to become a Canadian. She nice lady, but her son? Prince Tampioni! Pina suppressed a giggle as she recalled the nickname that the Italian press had for the Prince of Wales.

Settling back deeper into her chair she accidentally bumped the elbow of the young man beside her. "Excusee," she apologised, only to be treated to a scowl.

Stupid bitch can't sit still. Must have ants in her pants. Mihai Martel had learned that expression from his six-year-old nephew who attended kindergarten. They did not teach such things in his ESL class.

Thirty-four, a mechanical engineer by profession, Mihai had emigrated six–and-a-half years ago from his native Romania, now one of the poorest countries of Central and Eastern Europe. Immigration rules to the United States were too stringent and so, like many other Romanians his age, he had come to Canada. His brother Anton was already here and had been able to sponsor him.

At first it had been difficult for Mihai to get used to Canadian ways. He was repeatedly turned down for jobs in his field for not having "Canadian experience" and rejected for being "over-qualified" for lesser technician jobs. So he found odd menial work at gas stations and even worked as a janitor, until finally landing his current position in sales. But he was not happy. Didn't bust my f—ing butt at university for this. (By now he'd developed quite a flair for the English language).

It irked Mihai when people mistook him for a refugee. The term implied that you had jumped the queue or arrived here illegally without papers and were living off welfare, paid for by hard-working, over-taxed Canadians! F—ing Canadians can't tell the difference between Romania and Bosnia. And he wished he had a dollar for every time he'd been asked if he was a Serb or Croat.

Mihai had applied through the proper channels and waited four long years for them to evaluate his application. While they let the f—ing al Qaeda's and murdering Serbs in! He had also borrowed the equivalent of $20,000 from his mother to bring with him to Canada to support himself till he found a job. Yet some people just couldn't get the differences into their thick skulls and he was tired of explaining himself. F—ing lazy bum Canadians. Complain about everything and always blame someone else. They should be packed off to f—ing Romania. They wouldn't last a week.

The break he'd been waiting for finally came when he was accepted for a job in the Federal Government—pending citizenship of course. So here he was to swear loyalty to a foreign woman so he could get a job open only to Canadians. How ironic!

Mihai looked up at the impassive RCMP officer who towered beside the Judge on the dais. Sandy hair greying at the temples, his scarlet uniform added colour and majesty to an otherwise drab governmental room.

Sergeant Ian Campbell, however, felt anything but majestic or colourful. His feet hurt and he needed to take a leak badly. All that coffee.

From experience he knew that the ceremony would drag on for another half an hour or so. The oath was still to be administered and then the certificates would be distributed. After that he'd have to pose for endless photographs. How he hated that!

He noted fewer white faces in the room compared to the last time he was here. Gets fewer each time. Used to be towel heads and chinks. Now its camel jockeys and jungle bunnies. The few Europeans that do make it here are refugees from Chechnya or some other god-forsaken f—ing hell. Trouble-making bastards, all of them.

The Judge had switched back to English and Campbell frowned as he heard the words "equal opportunities for all." Equal for who Madame Judge, f—ing equal for whom?

He'd been overlooked for promotion twice for not being bilingual. Both times a junior francophone officer had superseded him while he was relegated to this desk job where he was expected to lend ceremonial presence to functions such as these. Where's the f—ing equal opportunity for white anglophone males, eh?

Looking down distastefully at the sea of faces, Campbell spotted a young Somali girl listening raptly to what the Judge was saying. Someone's taking all this seriously!

Fatima Mahdi was indeed taking it very seriously. She was moved by the ceremony, by the Judge, by the maple leaf flag, the RCMP officer and even the drab little court clerk who lurked in the shadows. So moved that she could not hold back the tears that were streaming down her cheeks. I'm going to be Canadian!

They'd arrived as refugees from Somalia, when Fatima was only nine years old. Rebel Bantus had burned down their village near Mogadishu and killed their father. The turmoil that followed was gruesome and Fatima worked hard at staying focussed on the kindness of the aid workers at the refugee camp. They had given her candy and called her beautiful.

Canada was so different from Somalia. Green and plush, with plenty of food for everyone. But there was a lot she had to learn and get used to. They

143

found an apartment on Bell Street where several other families from Somalia were also placed. Some were Bantus and this created tension.

She also found that some Canadians resented them for coming here. The man at the corner store glared at them as they passed by and hissed "Go back to where you came from you f—ing jungle bunnies." When she was younger Fatima would tremble when she he heard him say this, fearing that they'd be sent back to Somalia. Visions of fires, bombs, sirens and her poor father being stabbed to death, still haunted her.

Her boss at the Bank Street Bistro where she now worked part-time was not so polite, but she had learned to ignore his snide remarks for she needed the money. She was saving for University and then who knows? Perhaps medical school! On the whole, however, she found that most Canadians were kind and wished her well. She liked her teachers and the church group that had sponsored their family. She made friends and met kids from many different cultures. Some were refugees like her, and, like her, most were grateful to be safe in Canada.

Canada is a wonderful country, even if her brother Khalid did not think so. He was still so angry and spent his evenings on the street corner with other Somali men, plotting revenge on the Bantus.

"We don't belong here," he'd shout in Somali, when stoned. "They call us jungle bunnies and say we are warlords, cheating welfare. I hate it here. F—ing Canada."

Fatima had not told him that she had applied for citizenship. It would only upset him and cause tension in the house. And Allah knew that they had enough of that already. Only her mother knew she was here today, and had promised to celebrate with her later on.

"All rise," said the clerk. It was time for the oath. The moment they'd all been waiting for. Fatima tried to stand tall like the RCMP officer, but her feet were jellies. Tears streamed down her cheeks as she raised her right hand and solemnly swore allegiance to the Queen whose grandmotherly face looked down at her from the portrait on the wall. "Insh-Allah I'll be a good Canadian," she promised.

The Judge then instructed them to turn and greet their fellow new Canadians. Cheeks streaming with tears Fatima turned to the Indian-looking gentleman next to her. "Greetings", she sobbed grasping his outstretched hands in both hers. "Congratulations," he greeted back warmly, smiling at her exuberance.

"Congratulations," she whispered hoarsely to the Italian woman next to him who replied with equal emotion.

"Congratulations," she cried to the Chinese couple and they dimpled and nodded back at her.

"Congratulations, Congratulations, Congratulations," she repeated to the row of Sikhs who laughed back their greetings.

Even the rather sullen East European was infected by the moment and gripped her hand firmly as he shook it. They were now fellow Canadians.

Fatima climbed the dais to receive her citizenship card when the clerk called out her name. Giddy with exuberance she gushed, "Thank you, oh thank you," and burst into tears.

"There, there my dear," said the judge. Moved by the outburst she handed her a Kleenex from the box on her desk as the impassive RCMP officer stepped up and guided her efficiently back to her seat.

"I'm a Canadian now," she gushed at the Oriental family in the elevator going down.

"I'm Canadian now," she beamed at to the French Canadian security guard at the front of the building.

"I'm a Canadian," she told herself over and over again as she stepped into the cold street.

Feeling special, she hailed a cab. "Why not! I'm Canadian now!" she rationalized, settling into the warm interior of the Chrysler.

"Are you Somali?" asked the cab driver. The licence certificate taped to the back of the seat read "Ali Mahsuni Serif." He looks Turkish.

"No, I'm Canadian," she replied proudly showing him her citizenship card.

"Oh, I have one of those too," he laughed shaking his head, amused. "Makes no difference. You're still Somali."

About the Authors
and Illustrator

Cyril Dabydeen

Cyril Dabydeen has published over fifteen books of poetry, short stories, novels, anthologies, and over 100 book reviews and articles. He served on the jury of the Governor General's Award for literature (poetry) and on the Neustadt International Prize for Literature. Editor of the Journal of Caribbean Studies, his work was the subject of a book-length study and academic papers given in Canada, UK/Europe, Australia, and the US. His latest books include *North of the Equator*, fiction (Beach Holme, 2001) and *My Brahmin Days*, fiction (TSAR, 2000).

Angelo Eidse

Angelo Eidse has recently returned to his roots in Winnipeg after having lived on both coasts and points in between for most of the last decade. His writing explores the arcana of small-town life, the clandestine nature of relationships and the longing to belong. He is currently working on a collection of short stories.

Mark Foss

Mark Foss, a self-employed writer/editor, has worked in the field of international development since 1988. His fiction has appeared in various literary journals, including The New Quarterly. In 2001, CBC Radio's New Voices broadcast his first radio drama. He lives in Ottawa.

Sheila Howe

Sheila Howe holds a Bachelor of Science in Physiotherapy from the University of Western Ontario. Her articles have been published in *Canadian Living Magazine, Kingston Life Magazine, The Cottage Magazine, Canadian Homes and Cottages, FiftyPlus*, The Toronto Star and The Globe and Mail. She lives in an 1819 limestone house north of Kingston with her partner and three teenagers.

Timothy Kaiser

Originally from Saskatchewan, Timothy Kaiser is a member of the Saskatchewan Writer's Guild. He created his story "Mother Margaret and the Rhinoceros Café" out of a composite of characters he met while teaching in Black Lake, an isolated Dene community just south of the Northwest Territories border. The P.A. mentioned in the story is Prince Albert, a two-hour flight from Black Lake. Mr. Kaiser's writing has been published in Canada, the United States, and Asia. He teaches secondary school English Literature at the Canadian International School of Hong Kong.

Ken Loomes

Ken Loomes has been writing for many years, honing his skills with the Whodunit? Mystery Writers' group. The inspiration for this story comes from his teaching experiences on a reserve 200 kilometres north of Winnipeg. He now lives and works in Winnipeg.

Cecilia Kennedy

Cecilia Kennedy lives and writes in Brampton, Ontario, one of the most ethnically diverse cities in Canada. "Welcome to Mill Street" was a runner-up in the 2001 Toronto Star Short Story Contest. Her other stories have appeared in *The Grist Mill* and *Storyteller*, where she is a two-time winner of the Great Canadian Story Contest. Broken Jaw Press will publish a collection of her tales about a young Ontario provincial constable named Tony Aardehuis in Autumn 2003.

Rosemary McCracken

Rosemary McCracken is a Toronto journalist and teacher and has been published in *Room of One's Own* magazine. Rosemary's work with adult English-as-a-Second-Language students who inspired the characters in "Crazy."

James Romanow

When James Romanow returned to Canada after ten years abroad in Oman, Bermuda, and New York, he found that he had more in common with new immigrants than with Canadians. Most of his fiction is about what happens when the iceberg of Western culture grinds up against the peoples and lives of the developing world. His story "Incident on 33" was published in *Storyteller/Winter* 2003. "Mangohattan" appeared in *FreeFall Magazine*, Calgary. He now lives and works in Saskatoon.

Radhika Sekar

Radhika Sekar was born in India and has lived in Ottawa since 1974. She has taught in the Religious Studies departments of the University of Ottawa and Carleton University but now pursues her interest in creative writing. Her short stories have appeared in *Moving Fingers Write - an anthology* (2001, Mount Pleasant House) and *Brothers Borders and Babylon-a Canadian Perspective* (2001, Jervis Distributors). Sekar is the co-editor of this anthology.

Frank Symons

Completing a degree in English Canadian Literature and Film in Canada and Comparative Literature studies at the Sorbonne in Paris led somehow to a British Ph.D. in cyberspace geography and work in United Nations cross-cultural projects with colleagues from Africa, Asia, Europe and South America. After stints as a foreign correspondent and as English fiction reviewer at *Seix Barral*. (Barcelona and Buenos Aires), Symons returned home to a job with the federal government in Ottawa. He has published fiction and non-fiction in Canada, and Switzerland (UN/ITU), the UK and USA. Symons now lives in Perth Ontario. He also is co-editor of this anthology.

Illustrator

David Badour

Classically trained in many aspects of painting, drawing and commercial art, David has worked as an illustrator and graphic designer for seven years. During this time, he has used his skills in a variety of applications. These include book covers, newspapers, magazines, children's interactive games and web content. David has also worked as a conceptual artist and creative director for animation studios in Toronto and Ottawa. He now resides in Ottawa.

The Kaleidoscope Short Story Contest 2004
Ethnicity and Cultural Diversity

Do you have a story that relates to the dynamics of Canadian multiculturalism? .

We are looking for stories that show situations involving ethnicity, religious or cultural differences or reconciliations, and other social aspects unique to Canadian society.

If sufficient entries are of uniformly high quality, prize winning/honourable mention(s) will be published in the Kaleidoscope 2004 anthology.

Send $Cdn10 with 1st entry and $Cdn5 for each additional entry (same author), payable to Kaleidoscope Books by personal cheque or money order. 1st prize $150, 2nd prize $100, 3rd prize $50.

Open to Canadians and landed immigrants only.

Format required: double-spaced, pages numbered, one side, 8x11 paper, up to 5000 words, cover sheet with author's name, address, e-mail address (if possible), and telephone. No electronic submissions. MS not returned unless SASE enclosed. Submissions must be postmarked no later than July 30th, 2004.

Submitting authors agree to the decisions made by Kaleidoscope Books.

Send entries to **Kaleidoscope Books, RR#5, Perth, ON. K7H 3C7** For further details contact: **kaleidoscopebooks@rogers.com**

ISBN 141200542-6

9 781412 005425